BOUNCED

BOUNCED

TED STAUNTON

Scholastic Canada Ltd.
Toronto New York London Auckland Sydney
Mexico City New Delhi Hong Kong Buenos Aires

Scholastic Canada Ltd.
604 King Street West, Toronto, Ontario M5V 1E1, Canada

Scholastic Inc.
557 Broadway, New York, NY 10012, USA

Scholastic Australia Pty Limited
PO Box 579, Gosford, NSW 2250, Australia

Scholastic New Zealand Limited
Private Bag 94407, Botany, Manukau 2163, New Zealand

Scholastic Children's Books
Euston House, 24 Eversholt Street, London NW1 1DB, UK

www.scholastic.ca

Library and Archives Canada Cataloguing in Publication
Staunton, Ted, 1956-, author
Bounced / Ted Staunton.

Issued in print and electronic formats.
ISBN 978-1-4431-5717-9 (paperback).—ISBN 978-1-4431-5718-6
(html)

I. Title.

PS8587.T334B68 2017   jC813'.54   C2016-906158-2
                                                 C2016-906159-0

6 5 4 3 2 1   Printed in Canada 139   17 18 19 20 21

To the usual suspects

In the beginning, it was simple: I wanted to be a detective and I needed something to detect. How that led CC, Zal and me to everything that happened, and now to this — well, I'm hoping telling it will help me understand.

I'm also not sure what it means. Maybe nothing. Wiley Kendall asked me the other day if I'd learned anything from it all. Be careful what you wish for, is what I answered, but I'm not sure I believe that. If you were careful about wishes, there'd be no thrills at all.

CHAPTER

Borsalino Bounce

My career as a detective started with a bad bounce, so maybe I should start there. I'd gone with my friends Zal and CC to the Fidelity Bank on 3rd Avenue. Zal needed to get some birthday money out for a new ball glove, an Arturo Rocinante infielder's model, from Good Sports in the next block. The ATMs were down so he was in line with a lot of others, waiting for a teller. It was a hot Saturday in June and the bank was air-conditioned, so it was fine with me that sleeping turtles probably moved faster than Zal's line.

I was no stranger to banks. My Aunt Jenn, who I lived with, used to be a teller at one. CC had gone to a variety store to get a Popsicle. I waited in the cool inside the bank, by a table with free coffee laid on, passing the time with Zal's bouncy ball. That ball was pretty zingy, and even though I was being careful with it, just making little tosses, it got away from me and rabbited off across the bank's polished floor.

I spun after it and smacked headfirst into the middle of someone hustling toward the front doors. It was a soft middle. I grabbed the guy in a one-way hug to keep from falling over. He gave a little *oof* of surprise and we danced around for a second, my head in the armpit of his blue coat. I smelled the laundry soap they use on clothes you buy from the Goodwill and glimpsed a green-and-white tote bag from a local grocery in a gloved hand. Then he shook me off, and I stumbled on, yelping "Sorry!"

He was out the doors almost before I could turn around. I caught a glimpse of blue coat and ball cap behind people coming in, the guy kind of hunched over as if I'd hurt him. "Sorry," I called again, which was pretty useless.

A lady with a lemon-sucking frown handed me the bouncy ball. I was slinking back to my spot when another lady, dressed up and with a name tag, strode past with a set of keys and locked the doors.

Turning to everyone, she announced: "Sorry, folks, no cause for alarm, but we've just been robbed. The robber has already left the building. There's no danger. You may leave if you wish, but we ask you to stay if you can. Police are on their way. They may want statements from you."

Naturally, the whole place started buzzing. I hustled over to Zal. He hadn't seen a thing. "I was practising," he said. Zal showed me how he was walking a quarter across his knuckles. He wants to be either a magician or a major-league shortstop. It's all in the hands, he likes to say.

Listening to everyone else though, it didn't take long to realize the bank robber was the guy I'd bumped into. That gave me a little chill, I can tell you. Then, when someone said, "Borsalino Bandit," everyone was talking at once. The Borsalino Bandit had been robbing banks in our city for weeks. He was a bearded guy who wore a big hat to keep his face from security cameras. The cops were so frustrated they'd offered a fifteen-thousand-dollar reward.

"This guy didn't have a big hat," I said to Zal.

"He'd have to change things up a little." Zal squinted behind his glasses as he thought it over. "Or people would suspect him the moment he walked in. It stands to reason."

Zal had nothing to tell the cops, so he left to meet up with CC, who was peering impatiently in the window. We agreed they'd come back for me after he got the ball glove.

I knew I should wait for the police, and I wanted to. I was an important witness, maybe. Plus, it was exciting. I'd been reading a whack of detective stories and this would be a good chance to see how the cops operated — even though I knew from the stories that amateurs and private eyes were almost always smarter.

The police arrived a few minutes later. When they found out about how I'd bumped into the robber, one of them — Detective Yee — asked to take scrapings from under my fingernails, and a whole bunch of questions I really couldn't answer. Then her boss asked me the same stuff all over again. His name was Sergeant Castro. He was a flat-nosed, gum-chewing guy in a grey suit, balding, black-haired and not big, but he looked as if trucks would bounce off him.

"Duncan . . . Fortune?" He peered at the notes he'd been given. We were in someone's little office in the bank. "Why can't cops write neater?"

I didn't know why. Instead, I said again that I was almost thirteen years old and going into grade seven at Studies Institute, that I lived with my Aunt Jenn, why I was at the bank and that I hugged the bank robber.

"Studies Institute?" said Sergeant Castro. "Impressive." He didn't sound impressed. *Chew, chew, chew,* went his jaw. "You like it?"

"I don't know yet. I'm only starting there in September." Zal and CC were too. I didn't mention that.

He nodded. "Okay. Business." He squinted at the notes. "You didn't see the guy's face?"

"No, just his jacket. It was blue. I was chasing a ball," I explained. It sounded pretty lame. I added, "I think he had a blue cap. I saw that after. And he had gloves, leather work ones."

"And a shopping tote full of stolen money," Sergeant

Castro said, chewing some more. He sighed. "Well, we have other descriptions, including a green cap and a black one, and a brown one, but we'll get something from the cameras. Anything else come to mind? A fancy belt buckle? Shoes? A smell?"

"Laundry soap," I remembered, "from the jacket. Like the kind you smell on clothes from the Goodwill." I stopped. I didn't want Sergeant Castro thinking Aunt Jenn and I got all our clothes there. We didn't, just some. "And french fries, maybe." I hurried on, "He had a soft middle."

Sergeant Castro nodded glumly and worked his gum. "You're making me hungry. Well, on the bright side, no one got hurt."

"Was it the Borsalino Bandit?" I asked.

Sergeant Castro shrugged. "Wouldn't we all like to know. Could be a copycat."

"Is there really a fifteen-thousand-dollar reward?"

"That there is, Duncan, but I'm afraid your evidence is a little thin to qualify. Anyway, I doubt we'll be in touch again, but here's my card. Call the number on it if you think of anything else. And thanks for trying. I can tell you're the kind of kid who'd do his best to help us. Have fun at SI. I think you'll enjoy it."

"How come?"

"Went there myself. If they still have it, avoid the tuna noodle hot lunch."

Zal and CC were waiting outside. Zal was wearing his new glove. CC was pacing, in spite of the heat.

"Finally," she said. "What did you tell the cops?"

"There wasn't much to tell. Anyway, that's not important." The rest just spilled out: "That had to be the Borsalino Bandit. There's a big reward, right? I want to catch the Borsalino Bandit."

Balcony Bounce

But wait. I see now that to understand what happened next, I have to tell you about Studies Institute, *The World's Best 100 Detective Stories* and Lamar Del Ray. (I knew writing this was going to be hard.) I also see how Zal's bouncy ball linked everything together. Every bounce made a mark in a crazy connect-the-dots pattern of clues I didn't notice till it was too late. Maybe you'll see it before I did.

Okay, so. Studies Institute is a special school downtown, for smart kids, run by the university. Back in January, Miss Linton, our teacher at Park Lawn School, suggested to our families that CC, Zal and I should apply.

I could see Zal and CC doing that, they were total brainers. Zal, especially, was pumped. He did a little research and said not only was their computer science department super cool, he figured he could make the baseball team. Me, well, I wasn't so pumped. I didn't think I was a brainer; Miss Linton said I was "creative." She'd really liked this story I did before Christmas, about how I'd started to suspect about Santa way back in grade three, after we left a sandwich out for him Christmas Eve, and next morning I found peanut butter on Aunt Jenn's pillow. Later, I started writing my own story with the characters from *Zombiology*, and Miss Linton posted it for me on a fanfiction website and told me to keep writing.

When Aunt Jenn heard about SI, she was all over it. "Of course you're going, Skeets." She always called me Skeets or Skeeter. She said it was because when I was little I buzzed around like a mosquito all the time. Now she was doing the buzzing.

"But you have to pay to go there, and you always say that—"

"Money's tight," she finished for me, waving her fork. We were having dinner at the time. "And it is. It was tough when the bank let me go. You know that. But now that I'm working again things are getting better. Come spring I bet I can get lots of extra hours. And maybe Gram and Grandpa can kick in. I'm creative too, you know. And Miss Linton says there's a financial aid package we can apply for, and you'll have to help out. C'mon, you're going to write the entrance test and we're gonna go for it."

An entrance test? Money raising? Going downtown to school instead of around the corner? Becoming a brainer? This was turning into something bigger than I felt comfortable with. Truth to tell, I kind of liked life the way it was. "Why can't I just be smart at Park Lawn?"

"Because I don't want you doing what I did, getting bored and dropping out."

"No one drops out of grade six. I just don't want to go to a nerd school."

"You don't want to keep with CC and Zal? They're nerds?"

Well, yeah, they were kind of, but in a cool way. And I did want to stick with them; they were my best friends. Things were getting complicated. Aunt Jenn was a good arguer.

"Listen, Dunc. It's three hundred dollars just to write the test. This is not fooling-around stuff, kiddo. Promise you'll do your best, and I'll do my best for you." She arched an eyebrow over her iced tea. I promised. She put down her glass and smiled. Aunt Jenn had a smile so wide it could wrap around you. I'd seen it save her from speeding tickets too. She said, "But your best still won't beat me at cribbage."

"I have homework."

"Soon as you're done. I'll be shuffling the cards."

The entrance exam was in March. We all got in. I was amazed I made it. I think the only reason I did was because one choice for the essay question was *Describe and explain the best way to survive the zombie apocalypse.* I'd done a lot of thinking about that and had some good tips. I can tell you later if you want. (*See Appendix One.*)

Anyway, to celebrate, Aunt Jenn sprang for pizza, a movie and *The World's Best 100 Detective Stories*, a set of little hardback books with crumbly yellow pages that I'd found in the Goodwill. Aunt Jenn and I read a lot, but practically always books from the library, so owning these was special. "Just don't get any ideas," she kidded me.

The stories in *World's Best* were old but good. Whenever I read a good story I want to be like the hero, so for a little while I wished I was a brilliant detective, solving cool mysteries. But this was before the Borsalino Bandit, and our neighbourhood wasn't exactly a hotbed of crime. With nothing to detect, I decided to make up my own mystery instead. I was about done with zombies, and I even had a hero figured out: private eye Nick Storm, smart as a whip, cool as a cucumber and tough as nails. I know that is a lot of similes, but I found them in *World's Best* and they're exactly right.

Problem was, I had no mysteries for Nick Storm to solve, either. I was stumped. That's where the bouncy ball and Lamar Del Ray come into it. A few weeks later, on a warm Saturday in May, I was changing light bulbs for Wiley Kendall, the building super of the eight-plex we lived in. Getting paid for chores around the building was my way of helping save up for the SI fees. Wiley Kendall stood by my ladder, his big broom leaning against the wall. He was going on about his favourite subject while I worked fast as I could. His favourite subject was Aunt Jenn.

"That bank was nuts to let your aunt go, everybody's favourite teller." Aunt Jenn had worked in the B&G Trust branch in the local plaza.

"She likes her new job," I said, to cut it short. If I didn't, we'd talk again about how the bank manager fired Aunt Jenn because she "wasn't a team player."

"If your boss won't admit a rule is dumb, she's not worth working for anyway," Aunt Jenn told me at the time. These days, she drove a truck for Aurora B Nurseries.

"She deserved better," Wiley Kendall groused. "She bringing my order home with her tonight?" Now that Aunt Jenn was there, Wiley placed all his garden orders for the building with Aurora B.

"I guess. Done." I jumped down, bumping the broom. The metal handle hit the floor with a hollow clatter that echoed in my head. "Gotta go do science homework," I called, and ran for the stairs. I was expecting Zal and CC any minute. We had a project planned.

CC had gotten a new phone as her reward for getting into SI. Zal had gotten a new trick from a magic shop as his, and as a bonus, the bouncy ball: a rock-hard little planet of bright red something. "Zectron," Zal told us. "Ninety-two per cent coefficient of restitution." Zal loved that kind of stuff.

What it meant was it bounced like crazy. "Science

homework" was just our cover story. Really, we were going to make a YouTube video of bouncing the ball from my third-floor balcony. Zal had the ball and his fielder's glove, CC her phone and two fish-landing nets. Her family was all about outdoors stuff.

Snagging the rebound from a three-storey throw was tough, even with fishnets and a fielder's mitt. Filming was even tougher. That ball was wild. There was a deal of window rattling, ricochets off garbage bins and a close call with a chipmunk. Also a lot of yellow paint splotches after the ball hit the garden bench Wiley Kendall had painted that morning. It was a good thing he'd gone out jogging before we started.

"Man," Zal said, impressed. "You could knock yourself out with one of these." He had the ball in his scuffed old fielder's mitt.

"You could knock a *moose* out with one of those," CC said, waving her landing net. She would know. "My throw." She grabbed the ball. "Ready?"

I aimed the phone. The instant CC heaved the ball at the pavement, Zal yelled, "Wait!"

I saw some of the next part on the phone screen. The ball rocketed down as a rusty SUV and a cube van both pulled into the parking lot. The ball hit gravel, shot sideways, *BONGGED* high off the cube, smacked the hood of the SUV and caromed into the bushes, just missing a ground-floor window. Brakes squealed, a garbage bin toppled.

We all ducked back inside before anyone could spot us. Voices sounded down below. I peeked out. Two bearded men in big hats were standing beside their vehicles, looking up. The cube van had a logo: *Aurora B Nurseries*. Uh-oh.

"I better go down," I said. "You stay here."

By the time I got downstairs, Wiley Kendall had come puffing back from his jog. "That's crazy. Nothing falling off my roof," he was saying to the drivers.

"That's not a optic allusion," the SUV guy said, pointing at his hood. It wasn't the only dent, either. The rumble of the SUV's muffler almost drowned him out. Apart from his dark brown beard, everything about him was tan: workboots, cargo pants, baggy safari shirt and a cowboy hat with one side of the brim curved right up against the crown.

I walked slower. Wiley Kendall saw me. "You know about this, Duncan?"

"What? Oh, no, I was just, uh, looking for something."

"That fell?" His eyes narrowed behind his steamy glasses. He looked up. We all did. I saw now that the second landing net was dangling out our balcony rails. I also noticed I had streaks of yellow paint on my hands.

"Well, kind of." I shoved my hands in my pockets.

The SUV guy laughed and climbed back into his vehicle. A magnetic sign plate on the door hung a little crookedly. *Gator Aid*, it read. He said something out the window to Wiley Kendall that got lost in the muffler noise.

"Why you want to know?" Wiley Kendall said. "That's private information."

The SUV guy shook his head. He looked at me. The cube van driver looked at him. Wiley Kendall looked at them both. The SUV backed up and rumbled away.

Wiley Kendall shot me a *you were lucky* look and turned to the other driver. "Kendall?" the man said. His voice was a gruff whisper. His beard and moustache were black, his hat was a cowboy one too, only leather, with a flat, floppy brim all the way around. He had on mirrored aviator sunglasses. A stained blue bandana was knotted at his neck. "Delivery for you."

Wiley Kendall wiped his face. "Where's Jenn?" I wondered the same thing.

"Order desk. I'm deliveries today." He reached a clipboard out of the van. He was big bellied under one of those orange reflector vests. He had leather work gloves on. "Sign here."

Wiley Kendall frowned and signed. "What's your name?"

The man started, then coughed, "Lamar. Lamar Del Ray. Where you want it?"

The voice and mirrored glasses creeped me out. I was glad when he left. Things might have worked out better if he'd never arrived.

CHAPTER

World's Best Bounce

Zal and CC left too, when the coast was clear. CC had a saxophone lesson. Zal had to practise for a magic show at a seniors centre. I promised to get the ball back.

After lunch, Wiley Kendall had me repaint the bench, clean up paint spots and straighten the garbage bins. That ball had done a number, I can tell you. It had also disappeared. I searched a long time after Wiley went in, but didn't find it.

Then I swept the already-clean hallways. I figured that after what happened, Wiley Kendall might be extra picky, and I didn't want to get docked any pay. Clutching the broom handle, I remembered the hollow sound it made hitting the floor, and just like that a Nick Storm mystery idea popped into my head. Why then, I don't know. Who knows how you get ideas?

Anyway, by the time I finished sweeping I had it all worked out. Here's what it was: one night this museum caretaker has the alarm off while he sweeps. He gets knocked out and someone steals the famous Lamar diamonds. The cop, Inspector Chase, figures on international jewel thieves, but Nick Storm notices a bouncy ball in a far corner. Chase says some kid must have dropped it, but Nick's not so sure. He solves the case when someone bumps the caretaker's broom. It thuds, not clatters, and Nick instantly knows there's something in the hollow handle. Sure enough, it's the stolen jewels. The caretaker is the thief. He stashed the jewels in the broom and knocked himself out with the bouncy ball. It was supposed to bounce away, so no one knew how it happened, but it didn't bounce far enough.

Cool or what, huh? I even had a title: *Bad Bounce*. All I had to do was write it. I'd done enough for one day, though. I put away the broom and went up to our apartment, where I got a cold drink, turned on the radio and grabbed a *World's Best*.

When Aunt Jenn got home, the news was reporting a bank robbery in the east end. She didn't even take her boots off, just clomped in, snapped off the radio and turned to me. She had her tornado look in her eye. When Aunt Jenn got mad, which wasn't often, things swirled up fast. The storm didn't usually last long, but you remembered it. I guessed Lamar Del Ray had told her about something hitting the van. I should have thought of that.

I was almost saved by a knock on the door. It was Wiley Kendall. "*Ahem*, don't mean to intrude." Wiley Kendall did a lot of *ahem*ing around Aunt Jenn. Men tended to. It probably didn't help Wiley Kendall that Aunt Jenn was taller than he was too.

"What's up, Wiley?"

"Well, uh, you know me, Jenn: Wiley by name, not by nature. No, *ahem*, beating around the bush. Duncan was slinging this all over the place." He handed her the missing bouncy ball. "Couple of, *ahem*, complaints. Dented a car hood too."

"You don't say. Thanks, Wiley, much appreciated. I'll deal with this." She shut the door on him and the conversation. Not on me, though. "Disappointing, Skeets. I heard about this already. It was stump toad dumb, which is not your thing." She held up the ball. "What if you'd broken something and we had to pay damages?"

"What's a stump toad?" I asked.

"Don't change the subject. Kids going to Studies Institute are smarter than that. You apologize to Wiley?"

I nodded. "Yeah, sorry." She was right, but I was kind of mad at Wiley Kendall for ratting me out. He could have just given me extra work or something. I tried to change the subject again. "Who's Lamar Del Ray?" I thought I knew everyone at Aurora B.

"New. He keeps to himself." Aunt Jenn yanked her workboots off, letting them clunk to the floor. She marched into the kitchenette and got a beer. By now the tornado had pretty much blown out. "Anyway," she said, "lesson learned? We're smarter than this?"

I nodded again.

"All right then. Let's get to what we should be talking about." She put down her beer and walked back to the door. "Good news, Skeeter: Studies Institute is going to help some with your school fees. You got a bursary. They've sent us a cheque for three thousand dollars. That's why I was late. I stopped off to get this." She reached in her tote bag and handed me a phone, not a smart one, but still. "You're back in the loop, kiddo. And Monday I'll take the computer in and we'll get Internet back too."

"Wow, thank you." I held my new phone as if it were made of gold. This was huge stuff for us. Aunt Jenn's own cellphone was so old people asked to look at it. We'd had to drop TV and the Internet back when Aunt Jenn got let go by the bank. Our computer had a virus. We used the computers at the library instead. That was another reason we went there so much.

Aunt Jenn laughed and snatched the pizza menu from under its fridge magnet. "Try your phone. Anything but pineapple." I grinned. She said, "You know every student at SI is given their own laptop, Skeets?"

"Yeah, you told me before."

"Just do well, bud. I don't want you—"

"I'm not going to drop out."

"Good. With a real education you won't wind up like Grandpa, getting laid off all the time." Grandpa worked in a mine. I didn't know what I wanted to be but I didn't plan on being a miner. I didn't say that. She went to get her beer. "CC and Zal in on this today?"

I shrugged. She handed me the ball.

"Glad you didn't tell. A Fortune always takes one for the team." She took her beer out on the balcony. I guessed she was after a cigarette. Aunt Jenn tried not to smoke around me, but I knew she kept a pack in a little plastic container out there. Sometimes at night I'd hear her sneak out there after she thought I'd gone to sleep. This time she surprised me. She came back in with the pack and dumped it in the garbage. "And you know what, Skeeter? I can take one for the team too. I just quit smoking."

"Again," I said. I'd heard this before.

"Yeah, again. But this time think of the cigarette money I can save for SI. That'll motivate me. And on a more important topic, if you really want to have fun with one of those balls, find a school hallway with metal lockers on both sides. Wall ball. Throw hard for the top and see how many bounces you get wall to wall before it hits the floor. The *sound* is fantastic."

"How do you know?"

She winked. "None of your business, mister. Call it a mystery."

That reminded me of *Bad Bounce*. I ordered the pizza, then told Aunt Jenn my story.

"You are so right for that school, Skeets." She hugged me, I squirmed, and she went in to get cleaned up and make a salad. I wondered if SI would have a hall with metal lockers.

CHAPTER 4

Boyfriend Bounce

Things took a different kind of bad bounce the next day, when we went for groceries. A stained blue bandana was lying in the back of our old Toyota. "Hey," I said, "that Lamar guy—"

Aunt Jenn turned red as her hair. "I gave him a lift partway home." She stuffed the bandana in her pocket. "I better return it tomorrow. Say, did we get yogurt?"

We both knew we'd bought yogurt. You could tell she was avoiding something, and I had a bad feeling what it might be. If there was one thing Wiley Kendall and I agreed on, it was Aunt Jenn and boyfriends. Wiley Kendall didn't like them because he wanted to be one; I didn't like them, period. She hadn't had a boyfriend for a while, but all at once I suspected something was up with creepy Lamar Del Ray.

Over the next while, I was like Nick Storm on a case, hunting for evidence. Aunt Jenn didn't go on dates or get flowers, but her moods got wacky: sometimes she'd be all jazzed up, sometimes tired and grumpy. Mind you, she got that way every time she tried to quit smoking, but now it was worse. And every time I mentioned Lamar Del Ray, she'd change the subject. That said love to me, but I needed more proof.

Then other worries came bouncing in at all kinds of crazy angles. With the Internet back, there were emails from Studies Institute and I found out how much it cost to go there: twenty-five thousand dollars a year. That was a lifetime of me helping Wiley Kendall and way more than a three-thousand-dollar bursary. Aunt Jenn was working so hard. Could we do it? Even worse: If we did, what if I couldn't live up to that *best* she wanted for me?

To take my mind off things, I tried to write my mystery, *Bad Bounce*, but it turned into a worry too. I knew the story but I didn't know how to tell it. Where should it start? Who should tell it? How could I make the ending a surprise? If you want to see some ways I tried, I can show you those later too. (*See Appendix Two.*) *World's Best* detectives got to think about one problem at a time. I was swamped. You can see why I kept forgetting to give the bouncy ball back to Zal.

I guess he forgot too, because he never asked for it. We were all busy. Trout season opened and CC went north with her family most weekends. After school now, she practised fly casting into a tire in her backyard. Zal started baseball practice and went to a magic convention with his mom. I kept an eye out for signs of Lamar romance, puzzled over my story, went to the library and did extra chores for Wiley Kendall to keep from worrying even more about the money.

Aunt Jenn worked all the overtime she could get. Nights she worked late, I'd have dinner with Mrs. Ludovic, our neighbour next door. We'd watch the suppertime news and *Jeopardy!*, shouting out the answers. By now it was early June and the local news was reporting a string of bank robberies. The police suspected it was the same man each time. They were offering a reward of fifteen thousand dollars for information, calling him the Borsalino Bandit.

I didn't get it until Mrs. Ludovic explained: "*Borzaleeno* is big hat, fancy hat, like cowboys." She waved her hands around her head as we watched TV. *Borsalino* really suited her accent. Onscreen was a grainy shot of a hat and shoulders from a bank security camera. The wide brim of the hat hid the rest. Police said the robber had a beard and wore dark glasses.

One suppertime I was on Mrs. Ludovic's balcony, fiddling with the antenna for her, when a noisy muffler drowned out the TV. A dingy SUV I'd seen before pulled up across the street. This time the *Gator Aid* sign was straighter. The bearded driver looked across at our building. Our eyes locked.

"Dinner!" called Mrs. Ludovic, breaking the spell.

I stepped back. The SUV rumbled away.

I don't know why, but I texted Zal right off: *have your b ball*. My phone buzzed. Zal had texted: *Bring it Saturday. Ask can you come with me to get new ball glove*

The next bounce of the ball would start connecting the dots.

CHAPTER

Banjo Bounce

Of course, that Saturday was the robbery I already told you about. I'd called Aunt Jenn on my phone while I waited in the bank for the cops, but she hadn't picked up. She never did when she was on a delivery. When I finally reached her, she sounded flustered, and when I told her what happened, she flipped. I think she asked if I was okay four different times. Getting home that night, the first thing she did was hug me.

"Ohmygosh, Skeeter, I'm so glad you weren't hurt. Tell it to me again." I did, as she got us both iced teas. "You didn't see his face?"

I shook my head. "His armpit, mostly. And a ball cap. No one agreed on the colour. People said he had a beard and moustache."

"And the police think it was this Borsalino Bandit?"

"Sergeant Castro didn't say. He said it might be a copycat."

Aunt Jenn shuddered. "I just think of you barging into him. He mustn't have known what to think. What if he'd had a gun?"

"Does the Borsalino Bandit use a gun?" I asked.

Aunt Jenn paused. Then she shrugged. "I guess I just figured there wasn't a gun because he didn't use it. What did the sergeant say?"

"Just that nobody was hurt."

"Amen to that. Skeeter, I'm too shook up to think, let alone make dinner. If anything had happened to you . . . Oh my. Let's get burgers. And a movie, a funny one."

You probably noticed the one thing I didn't tell Aunt Jenn: that I wanted to catch the Bandit. Partly I was scared she'd forbid it, because she worried about me so much. Partly I thought it would be cool to surprise her with the reward money. Mainly, as Zal, CC and I realized riding home on the bus, none of us really had the faintest idea how to catch a bank robber who was baffling the cops. So much for being like Nick Storm. No wonder I was having trouble with my story.

We'd agreed that Zal would find out everything he could about the Borsalino Bandit online and that I'd ask Aunt Jenn about bank robberies, since she used to work in a bank.

"Then I'll figure it all out," CC had proclaimed. That's when Zal rolled his eyes and gently dropped the bouncy ball on her head. We'd had to scramble around the bus to find it.

I couldn't seem to find the right time to ask Aunt Jenn that weekend. Monday, she was working late again. Mrs. Ludovic asked me to make a grocery run for her: two cans of mushroom soup. I didn't mind going. I coasted down the hill to the plaza on my bike, rolled past the Goodwill where I found *World's Best* and the B&G Trust branch where Aunt Jenn used to work, and that's when I saw the sign:

OPENING SOON
GATOR AID WEST
HERPETOLOGY HAVEN
MEETING ALL YOUR
SNAKE & REPTILE NEEDS

It was in the window of a vacant store two doors down from the bank. I scanned the parking lot for the noisy SUV: nothing. Inside the store was a jumble of boxes and tools. A couple of the cheesiest fake palm trees you've ever seen framed the window.

I hit the supermarket for Mrs. Ludovic and hustled back up the hill. I wanted to double-check *herpetology* before I called CC about this. If anyone had "snake and reptile needs," or wanted to have them, it would be her.

But I didn't want to get caught out on anything. Everyone remembered how she'd gotten our last year's teacher on whether koalas were bears.

Online I found out herpetology comes from the Greek word *herpo*, to creep, and *herpetan* was the Greek word for reptile. This was the kind of stuff I needed. I called and told her about the sign and the store.

"Sweet," she said. "I can't go check it out now, though. I've got my banjo lesson."

"I thought it was saxophone," I said.

"I switched. Anyway, tell Zal. We'll go right after school tomorrow. Maybe we can get a cobra or something for his magic act."

"It only said 'opening soon,' C."

"Better early than late. You never can tell." She hung up. I headed to Mrs. Ludovic's.

Bullfrog Bounce

The next afternoon, we all rode down to the plaza. A new sign hung in the Gator Aid window: *Grand Opening Saturday.* Now a counter display case was stocked with merchandise, and lights glowed in big glass boxes.

"Terrariums," CC announced. "Hope there's venomous snakes. Baby Komodo dragons would be cool. You've got to get a king cobra or a python, Zal. Imagine pulling one out of your hat."

"The rabbit is enough trouble," Zal said. "*You* get a cobra."

"I'm asking for sure on Saturday," CC said. "C'mon, let's hit the Trails."

The Trails were the best riding around. They were

in Oakwood Park, the biggest park in our city. Our neighbourhood bordered its west side. The Trails ran through some killer hills that were also excellent for winter tobogganing.

I bet I knew why CC wanted to go there. Coming down the last hill, you went past Green Pond. CC always liked stopping there because of what she called its "ginormous amphibian density." In other words, the place had lots of toads and turtles.

I guessed that if Gator Aid wasn't open, she was going to see what she could find herself. What the heck, I thought, if we couldn't catch a bandit, maybe she could catch a bullfrog.

Green Pond was usually deserted, but now when we rode up people were clustered at the edge. Parked nearby was a van marked *Municipal Animal Control.* Everyone was murmuring and staring at the water. We edged closer.

"What is it?" Zal asked.

A lady turned to us. "There's an alligator in there."

"Alligator? Where?" CC went up on her toes.

The lady pointed. I squinted. Green Pond was called that for a reason. It was dark green with a topping of light green scum, and shadowed most of the way around by trees that seemed about to topple into the water. The weird part was that past the trees on the far side, where you'd expect a wilderness, was a road and houses. The SUV with the *Gator Aid* sign was parked there.

The sunny part of the pond was choked with bulrushes. A slimy log poked above the surface, barely floating. Beside it, I finally spotted two dark little bumps in the scum. Not far behind them, looking like ripples on the surface, were two rows of wavy lines.

"It was sunning on the log," the lady explained. "But when the van pulled up, it slipped into the water."

"It can't be very big." CC sounded disappointed.

"Give him twenty years, he'll grow on ya," said someone, and I recognized the bearded SUV driver. Now he had on a wide-brimmed straw hat. I eased back a little. "Technically," he went on, "it's a caiman, spectacled caiman. Looks a year old maybe, just a baby."

"How big will it get?" CC pushed forward.

"About six, seven feet; three hunnerd pounds." He turned and grinned through his beard. "If he was home in South America, that is." He wore a little shell on a rawhide loop around his neck.

A lady in a blue uniform shirt said, "Big or small, Animal Control can't deal with it. We're not trained for this. I don't even have anything to put him in. The department will have to find someone that can handle it."

"Look no further," said the driver. "This just happens to be my business." He dug some business cards out of a pocket in his safari shirt and passed them around. "Marty Raymond," he said. "Gator Aid. Chief herpetologist. Got a regional outlet opening over at the plaza on Saturday, in fact. That's why I was in the neighbourhood."

People looked at the cards, then back at Marty Raymond, impressed. "I'll round up some gear and get him tomorrow afternoon."

"Tomorrow?" someone said.

Marty Raymond nodded at the pond. "That little guy's not going anywhere. You want to do it right, and safe, for him and me. He's lost and scared, doesn't need any more stress. And I don't want to get bit. He may be little but he's got teeth like razor blades." He tipped his hat back. "One o'clock tomorrow, if you care to take in the show."

People began to chatter and move away. Some shuffled closer to the pond and got video with their phones.

"I'll report that and be here tomorrow," said the lady from Animal Control, waving the business card. "It's our jurisdiction. One o'clock?"

"The more the merrier," said Marty Raymond. "See you then." He raised his voice, "Heck, bring your friends."

A couple of people swung their phones to get a shot of him too. He flashed a big grin again, then lifted his own phone and started tapping something in. As he did, he said to us without looking, "You three gon' be here? You could help. I'll need assistants I can count on."

"Won't you bring helpers with you?" Zal asked. "Like, from Gator Aid?"

"We're short-staffed right now, pardner. I can't bring people in just for this, what with travel and all. Can you help?"

"I'm in," said CC.

Zal said, "We could film it. Right, C?"

Marty Raymond nodded. "Video would be huge. And I'll need a paddler. Excellent." He talked as if we'd been a team all along.

"Um," I said. "We've got— What about school?"

Marty Raymond turned to me and nodded. "Good point. I could tell you three were smart. That's why I spoke to you. Son — what's your name?"

"Duncan."

"Duncan, you can sit in science *class* any day or you can live science, like I do. This is the real thing, wild-life biology right here. Besides, when you gonna get the chance to catch a gator again?"

"Caiman," CC corrected.

"Beg pardon. Precision pays. You three are definitely the kind of helpers I'll need. Duncan, you choose what's best for you. Bring the whole darn class for all I care. More the merrier. Can't do it, I understand, but I'd surely appreciate your help." He winked. "Comes to it, there's worse in life than skipping a little school. I didn't say that. Hope to see you tomorrow."

He shook hands with Zal and CC, then me. He had a strong grip. As we shook, he stared hard at me for an extra second. I wished I hadn't sounded wussy about school.

"Tomorrow," CC called as we rode off.

Marty Raymond was already texting.

Both Sides Bounce

Do you think Miss Linton will bring us?" I puffed. It was uphill riding home.

"Naw," Zal sighed. He swung off his bike and started to walk it. "She'd have to do parent consent forms and all that." Zal's parents were teachers, so he knew those kinds of things. "I wish we could, though. It would be so cool."

"So let's go anyway," CC said. "Who's going to know?"

"You mean skip off school?" Zal stared. "We'd get in trouble."

"I bet my dad would let me."

"Well my parents would go ballistic," Zal sighed.

"Not if we do it right." It took a heartbeat to realize it was me who'd just said that. I didn't even know why I had, except a spark had flared. It was as if Marty Raymond had dared me with that handshake. I hurried on, "Look at it this way: Have we ever skipped before? Have we ever even been late? Who's going to suspect? We're the goodies."

And we were. It wasn't like we got noticed for it much. Sure, there were always a couple of guys who'd ask Zal to make himself disappear after the school talent show, and CC's smart mouth got her into trouble sometimes, mostly with other girls. She hadn't done herself any solids when she'd brought a stuffed animal to school for favourite things day in grade four. Not a plush toy; a real squirrel she'd stuffed with her dad's help. It was lumpy in odd places and the eyes seemed to look in different directions. That got the girls saying CC was weird. Of course, CC *was* weird, but in a good way. Most of us guys were impressed by a girl who fished, camped and had a good throwing arm. Plus she punched the one guy who laughed at the squirrel and you could tell it hurt. As for me, I mostly just played along. Until now. Now I wanted like anything to break the rules.

"It would be so much cooler than school," CC said.

Zal thought this over too. "Yeah, but how do we do it?"

Somewhere in *World's Best* it says that detectives and crooks think the same way. Maybe that's why we figured it out so fast. "This better work," Zal said.

"Don't worry," I said, "it's not like they can kick us out. We're already going to another school."

"How about we get grounded forever? I don't want to mess up ball season."

"Come on, Zal," CC snorted. "As long as we're home on time, how are they going to find out?"

The plan was simple. All you needed to get out of class was a note from home or a call to the school. CC couldn't ask for permission in case her folks blabbed to Zal's parents or Aunt Jenn, so she'd get her older brother in high school to make the call and pretend to be her dad. His voice was deep enough, and if you called before eight o'clock in the morning you just had to leave a voicemail, with a thousand others. Then CC would call the school before eight too, and fake being Zal's mom. She'd say he needed to be excused at lunch to see his grandpa, who was sick. They couldn't phone for me too, so I'd write myself a note.

I used our now-fixed computer and my best letter-writing style that I'd learned in class:

June 17

Dear Miss Linton,

Please excuse Duncan from class at lunchtime today, as he has a dental appointment this afternoon at the dentist.

Hoping this finds you well,

Jenn Fortune

I spelled *appointment* wrong but the spell-checker on the computer caught it. The only tricky part was copying Aunt Jenn's signature onto the bottom. Sergeant Castro probably would have called this "forging," but I told myself a note for school wasn't important enough to count.

I hunted around for something she'd signed and found a cheque with the phone bill on the hall table. She never paid anything with a credit card or online. "Teller training," she'd say. "I like a paper trail." I held the cheque against the glass door to the balcony to get the light behind it, then carefully traced her signature onto a sheet of printer paper. I practised a few times, fast, on the same page, then signed the note. It looked pretty good. I put back the cheque, folded the note and put it in my backpack, tore up my practice sheet and flushed it down the toilet. Now I was on both sides of the law.

CHAPTER

Bump Bounce Boogie

Next morning, I made sure to hand my note to Miss Linton while she was talking to someone else, so she might not take time to look too closely at it. Sure enough, she just said, "That's fine, Duncan. Is anyone picking you up or are you going home first?"

"Going home."

"I hope you have no cavities." She turned back to the other kid.

As I walked to my desk, I let out the breath I'd been holding. Man, I thought, if I'd known it was this easy . . .

Heading to Oakwood Park, though, I got nervous again. It felt strange to be out in the middle of the day, as if I were wearing a sign that read *Kid Ditching School*.

I tugged my ball cap low and hustled along. I was

across the street from the park, waiting to cross, when an old silver Toyota like ours came zipping along. Instantly I thought Aunt Jenn had found out and was after me.

I ducked behind a trash bin, felt stupid and stood up in time to see it *was* our car — I could tell by a ding in the passenger door — but it wasn't Aunt Jenn driving. It was a bearded man with sunglasses: Lamar Del Ray. My stomach did a little flip. The car's turn signal flashed and the Toyota scooted into the park drive. Lamar Del Ray drove even faster than Aunt Jenn.

For a moment I forgot all about caimans and skipping school. Was this the proof I needed about Aunt Jenn and Lamar Del Ray? Or was there an explanation? The traffic cleared and I dashed across the street and into the park. I was tempted to try and follow the car but the park was big and the Toyota was already long gone. I whipped out my phone to call Aunt Jenn. In the nick of time I remembered that I'd have to explain to her why I was at Oakwood Park when I was supposed to be in school. Finding out about this was going to take some planning, and right now we had a caiman to catch.

I checked the time while I had the phone out: almost one o'clock. I stuffed it back in my shorts pocket and hurried to Green Pond.

It didn't feel as much like a jailbreak when I met up with Zal and CC. A small crowd had already gathered. Animal Control was there, and a police cruiser. The only person who wasn't there was Marty Raymond.

A few minutes later, he rolled up in the noisy SUV. "Sorry, folks. It's been a busy one. Hey, there's my support team."

That was us. Marty Raymond swung us into action. We helped lower a cage like a big cat carrier from the back of the SUV, then a longer, sturdier version of the fisherman's landing net CC had brought to my place for the bouncy ball experiments, life jackets and an inflatable dinghy. We took turns pumping up the dinghy while Marty Raymond scouted the pond.

As we capped the air valve he came back to us. "Okay, Gator Aiders. Got the camera?"

CC nodded and held up her phone. "Zal films, I paddle. It's my specialty."

"What about me?" I said, feeling left out. After all, if I hadn't had the idea for skipping, we wouldn't be here.

Marty Raymond turned to me. "Ready to net?"

"What?" I said.

"Net means wet. Can you take it?"

"How do—"

"I'll do it!" CC jumped in.

"No, ma'am, we need a steady hand on the paddle." He looked back at me. "You in, Duncan?"

Somehow it was important that Marty Raymond, Gator Aid Guy, had remembered my name. "I'm in," I said, and unslung my backpack.

"Then let's boogie." He looked around. "Not everyone's here but we can get started." He called over the Animal

Control workers and the police officers. I wondered if the cops would ask us why we weren't in school, but they didn't. The rest of the crowd trailed behind.

"Simple plan, folks," Marty Raymond said. "PCC: patience, calm, quiet."

"Quiet doesn't start with *c*," CC sniffed.

Marty Raymond didn't miss a beat. "Patience, calm, *control*. First off, we locate the critter, then I go in after him with my support team here. Thing to remember is, he's jumpy, prob'ly missing his mom. Commotion will make him harder to catch. It'd be nice to get this done in time for . . ." His voice trailed off as he looked around the park again. "Anyway, let's get at it. Spread out nice and quiet around the perimeter and look hard. No shouting or rushing."

Everyone did as they were told. I stood at the edge of the pond, half hoping nobody spotted anything. I didn't know exactly what I'd be doing, but I didn't like the sound of what I did know. As we looked I heard more cars pull up, but I didn't turn around. Traffic rolled past outside the park.

Finally, a lady with binoculars broke the quiet. "Got him." She pointed to the middle of the pond, where the dark green was blanketed by light green scum. Dark bumps rode the surface. You could just see the side of the caiman's head.

CHAPTER

Bottoms-Up Bounce

"**B**ingo," Marty Raymond said. "PCC. Leave it to Gator Aid." He turned to us. "Life jackets on. I go in first. Launch the boat quiet from over there when I'm well away from shore. Don't come near, just keep it steady and film. Me and the caiman. And my face, not the back of my head. Got it? Okay."

Zal and CC headed off.

The police had their own inflatable boat. Marty Raymond told them to stay back too. Then he handed me the last life vest and the landing net.

"Duncan, my man, you're backup. I go in there," he pointed. "You give me a good head start, then ease in over the other side."

"Right in front of him?"

"A gator's got two blind spots, right in front and right behind. I sneak up behind. You stay dead in front of him and keep the pole flat, ahead of you, just under the water. Go real slow and quiet, he won't see you or know you're there. If I signal, pull the net *up*, because if our buddy spooks he'll dive, and go right into it."

I looked at my shorts and sneakers, then at Green Pond. It had never looked swampier. "You mean we're just going to wade in?"

"Why not? Cops say it's not very deep. 'Sides, you got a life jacket on."

"But what if—"

Marty Raymond knelt and retied one of his hiking boots. He gave me a long sideways look and whispered, "Nothing to it, pardner. He's the scared one. Most he'll do is scoot away from us. Just stay cool, look as if you know what you're doing and leave the heavy lifting to me. Got it?"

I nodded in spite of myself.

"Main thing is, we give 'em a show." He stood up and said, "Let's do it."

"Wait a minute," someone said. "Surely you're not letting those kids—"

"Sir," Marty Raymond said, "*those kids* can deal with this better than most adults. They're trainers in Gator Aid's Kids and Critters program and they know more about handling reptiles than these folks do." He waved a hand at the police and Animal Control officers.

"Situations like this are standard procedure, a certificate requirement. Now if you'll kindly stand back and keep the noise down, we'll get 'er done."

I moved to my spot. Marty Raymond moved to his and stepped into Green Pond. He moved so carefully the water barely rippled. When he got waist-deep, he waved to Zal and CC. They gently set the dinghy on the water, climbed in and quietly pushed off.

It was so still, for a moment the only sound you could hear was the single dip of CC's paddle. Out on the road, a car rolled by. Marty Raymond waved to me.

I took a deep breath and stepped in. Water flooded my sneakers. I edged forward. The bottom sucked at my feet. The water was so murky I couldn't see my feet by the time my knees were wet. Weeds — or something — clutched at my bare legs and I wished I'd worn jeans. I tried not to think about what might be down there and concentrated on not making ripples.

The pond got deeper faster than I expected. At waist-deep I slipped the net and pole into the water ahead of me, just under the surface, the way Marty Raymond had said. The bumps of the caiman's eyes and snout sat on the green scum like gunsights, maybe twenty yards away. I was right on target.

I looked at Marty Raymond. He nodded.

The caiman hadn't moved. We eased in farther. I felt the life jacket begin to bob. Marty Raymond was chest-deep in the blanket of scum now, about thirty feet back of the caiman. I was at the edge of the stuff. It was so thick you couldn't see the net and pole just under the surface. I could feel the bottom dropping off steeply and I couldn't go farther without the life jacket floating me off my feet.

I stopped and stared hard at those dark little bumps. They were so still I wondered if the caiman was really there. It had to be there. Because if it wasn't there, where was it? *That* was a thought I didn't need. I clutched the pole tighter.

Then Marty Raymond sank slowly, arms stretched in front of him, until only his head seemed to bob on the surface, a hat-wearing balloon.

There was no sound. His head drifted closer and closer. Ten feet back. The caiman didn't move. Nine feet, eight feet . . . I thought, *teeth like razors.* Six feet . . . five . . . four . . .

Thwup.

There was a little swirl of water, and the caiman was gone. Then Marty Raymond rose, arms high, holding a three-foot-long gator. One hand was clamped right behind its head, the other gripped the caiman's tail just back of the hind legs.

I heard applause from the shore. Marty Raymond flashed a huge grin and turned to Zal's camera. A second beard of green algae hung from his regular brown one. His neck and shoulders were draped in a scarf of weeds.

CC angled the dinghy closer as Zal filmed.

"Get the crowd too," Marty Raymond ordered, holding the caiman like a trophy. "Gator Aid to the rescue," he called, then stepped forward and vanished.

For an instant, all that was left was his straw hat, floating on the surface. Then it was joined by a caiman that shot up out of the water in my direction and belly-flopped with a splash.

I yelled. My feet slipped and I toppled backward, jerking up the landing net. It came alive. As the life jacket caught me, I saw the caiman airborne, struggling in the net. Let's just say I held on tight.

Then a weedy Marty Raymond was honking and spluttering beside me. "All right, pardner, I got him." He took the pole and hoisted the caiman higher. "A wrangler in action," he called. "Training pays off. Let's give it up for Duncan here."

There was more clapping as we waded to shore. Marty Raymond puffed and swore under his breath all the way, his sopping safari shirt clinging to a good-sized beer gut. "They didn't tell me there's a deep spot."

CHAPTER

Backfire Bounce

CC and Zal followed us, with Marty Raymond's soggy planter hat. He slapped it on his head before easing the caiman out of the net and holding it up again, trophy-style, and showing it to the crowd. Cameras were clicking.

A man behind a big video camera leaned in. A dark-haired woman with a microphone stepped up to Marty Raymond. "Think we'll make six o'clock?" he asked her.

"Probably," she laughed. "Eleven and tomorrow morning for sure. It's a great story."

That was when I understood what he'd been waiting for earlier: news photographers and crews from the TV stations.

Marty Raymond started talking into the microphone

about how the caiman was probably a pet somebody had left here when it got too big.

"Hey, we're going to be on TV," CC whispered happily.

"Great," Zal groaned. "So much for secretly skipping school."

We all looked at each other.

"Let's get out of here," I said.

It was too late. A video camera swooped in, and another lady with a microphone said to us, "Great work, guys. Was it scary?"

We all shrugged and tried to look away. It was hard to know what to say.

"But you're all trained to do this, aren't you? That's quite amazing."

All I could think was that if I didn't act like me, maybe no one would believe it *was* me.

I said, "Oh yeah, we do this lots. It took five years to learn."

"Five *years*?" The lady was amazed. "You must have been very young."

"Hey," I said, nodding at CC. "She stuffed her first squirrel in grade three." I pointed at Zal. "This guy's hands are faster than snakes."

"Wow," said the lady. "That's truly impressive. What are your names?"

"Nicole Storm," CC said promptly. I'd told her my mystery idea.

"Arturo Rocinante," said Zal.

"Like the Yankees shortstop?" The lady knew her baseball. Zal nodded.

She turned to me. I said, "Lamar Del Ray."

Marty Raymond's head snapped around.

"Are your parents here, kids?" the reporter asked. "We have to get their permission to air your interviews."

"Well, no," I said. "They're all at the detective agency solving some jewel and bank robberies."

She nodded. "I'll get back to you about reaching them." She and the cameraman turned away.

"Whew," CC said. "Good thinking. We might be safe."

We all did high-fives but I knew I wasn't going to be safe until I got home and dealt with my soaking wet clothes.

"Let's go," I said. We took off our life jackets.

Marty Raymond was saying, ". . . Luckily we're opening a new outlet in this neighbourhood and I just happened by yesterday . . ."

We headed for our backpacks. As we hoisted them, Marty Raymond said something to the reporter and hurried over to us, still holding the caiman. It had a dribble of algae hanging from its snout. Otherwise it looked quite calm.

"Thanks, pardners," he said. "Great get. This is gonna launch Gator Aid with flying colours on Saturday. You can email me that video? Wanta run it on continuous loop in the store window. Great publicity."

"Lucky for you someone dumped their pet," CC said.

Marty Raymond winked. In a lower voice he said, "Maybe lucky for me there was a pond close by that a, uh, Gator Aider could slip one of his little buddies like Chester here into for a day or so." He nodded at the caiman in his hands.

"You mean—" Zal said.

"Tricks of the trade," Marty Raymond smiled. "We all gotta eat. Now listen, come on down on Saturday, we'll do it up right. Now, I know those weren't your real names. Thank you—"

"CC."

"Zal."

"And you're Duncan," he said to me. He looked as if he was about to say something else, but he didn't.

I nodded.

Solemnly he said, "Thank you, CC, Zal and Duncan."

Solemnly we all said, "You're welcome." It's easy to be solemn when a caiman is being held close to your face, even if it does look calm.

Marty Raymond must have caught on because he laughed and lifted Chester away. "Hey, you guys, it's been a slice. See you Saturday, I hope. And drop in any time."

"I will," I called as he hustled back to the TV crews.

I squelched with every step we took. "What time is it?" CC asked. I reached for my phone and stopped in mid-squelch. Oh no. I pulled my phone out of my soggy pocket and pressed the button. The screen stayed blank. As I stared, Zal said, "Just after two."

Barely an hour had gone by. In that time I'd skipped school, seen Lamar Del Ray in Aunt Jenn's car, caught a caiman, gotten soaked, lied to stay off TV and wrecked my phone. I was thinking it couldn't get much worse as a silver Toyota whisked by. Lamar Del Ray wasn't driving it anymore, unless he'd become a red-haired woman. Aunt Jenn. The Toyota did a rolling stop at the park entrance and vanished in the city traffic.

Brown Rice Bounce

When Aunt Jenn got home, I was in the comfy chair pretending to read "The Blue Cross" in volume four of *World's Best*. I'd run my clothes and shoes through the dryer in the basement laundry without being caught by Wiley Kendall. I was pretty sure Aunt Jenn hadn't seen me in the park, and if she had I'd try to *brazen it out* as they'd say in a story.

But I was worried just the same. I was even more worried about two other things. One was my phone. Cover off, it was stuffed into the bag of brown rice in the kitchen cabinet. CC and Zal had said that the rice would draw the water out and maybe save it. The other was Lamar Del Ray. How could I find out about him without giving away where I'd been?

Aunt Jenn came in with a tired smile and a couple of grocery bags. Her green-and-yellow Aurora B golf shirt had a streak of dirt on one shoulder. She wrestled off her workboots and socks and wiggled her toes. The nails were painted bright red. "Now there's relief." She padded past me into the kitchenette with the bags.

I kept my eyes on the book. I heard the tap run, plastic rustle, the clunk of tins and cupboards and the soft thud of the fridge door.

Aunt Jenn called, "Skeets, it's the kind of a day when you can't decide if a shower or a beer comes first."

What would Lamar choose, I wanted to say, but that didn't exactly sound subtle. "Toss a coin," I said instead. My voice came out sounding as if one of Marty Raymond's snakes were tightening around my neck.

Aunt Jenn didn't seem to notice. "A cool one it is," she said. I heard footsteps behind me and the *snick* of a pull tab. "Did you like your lunch today?" Aunt Jenn asked.

I almost fell out of the chair. I hadn't had time to eat my lunch, and I'd forgotten to ditch it. Where was my backpack? Before I could move, someone started pounding on the door and yelling. I did fall out of the chair. I felt mist go past my head as beer sprayed across the living room. A few drops darkened my wrinkly shorts. I saw some dried algae there as well.

"Who is it?" Aunt Jenn spluttered.

There was more pounding. The yelling had a familiar accent. Mrs. Ludovic burst in the instant Aunt Jenn turned the door handle. "Iss Dungcan, Dungcan," she cried. "Dungcan iss on TV!"

She dragged us across the hall. The news was blaring. I wondered if I could somehow get to the balcony and twist the aerial, but it was too late. The picture of Oakwood Park was perfect. The dark-haired lady who'd tried to interview us was yammering into the camera, while behind her, the crowd milled at the pond. Zal, CC and I were smack in the middle of the shot. Next came Marty Raymond getting ready to go in the water, us in the pond, catching the caiman, and Marty Raymond jumping up with it.

At first, Aunt Jenn looked puzzled as she watched. A smile twitched for a microsecond. That turned to a frown as things happened in the pond. And then, as the cameras closed in tight on Marty Raymond and he started talking, everything changed. Aunt Jenn caught her breath. Her face went pale under her freckles.

The picture cut to the news anchor, who said, "Wow, no swimming for me. Up next: the Borsalino Bandit strikes again."

Aunt Jenn had tuned out; it was tornado time.

"This is that place at the plaza?" she said. She stomped out of Mrs. Ludovic's and came back with shoes and car keys. "Right, let's go." She grabbed my shoulder and marched me downstairs and out to the car.

We burned rubber pulling out and zoomed down the hill. The Gator Aid SUV was parked in front of the store.

Aunt Jenn stopped crossways behind it, hemming it in. "Wait here." She jumped out, leaving the motor running, and stormed to the shop door, pounding on it when it wouldn't open. She started yelling the moment Marty Raymond let her in, barging through the doorway and into the place, finger pointing.

I couldn't see very well from where I was sitting, but despite my track record for the day, I was smart enough not to get out of the car. I caught fractured glimpses of yellow and green and arms waving behind the fake palm trees and I could hear the sound, if not the words, of Aunt Jenn yelling. Then she was steaming back out to the car. She slammed it into gear and we screeched away across the parking lot.

"Don't you ever go near that man or that place again." Aunt Jenn didn't look at me as she spat out the words.

"But, it wasn't really that danger—"

"No buts."

"The gator was the scared one." That was only partly true, but whatever it was about Marty Raymond that had convinced me to skip school was making me stand up to Aunt Jenn too.

"Never mind gators. *That man* is trouble, you hear? Trouble. Stay away."

"Do you know him?"

"I know enough. I don't want to know any more, and neither do you. Stay away."

Angrily, I blurted, "If you stay away from Lamar Del Ray."

"What?"

"I saw him today, driving your car into the park. And later you drove it out."

Aunt Jenn slammed on the brakes, jerking us forward against the seat belts. She turned to me. "I don't know what you're talking about. I went to the park at lunch and took a walk. Alone."

"He was driving your car."

Behind us, a horn honked. Aunt Jenn sank back in her seat. The horn honked again. She reached out her window and flipped a finger. "You didn't see that." She gunned the car up the hill to home.

By the time we pulled in, the tornado was over. As we got out of the car, she said, "All right, Skeeter, I owe you an explanation. I wasn't going to mention it, because I can tell you don't care for Lamar. I don't much either. I only deal with him when I have to. But he asked to borrow the car today to go to a job interview somewhere else, thought it would look better if he drove up instead of riding the bus. So I loaned it to him while I went for a walk. Truth to tell, I felt sorry for him 'cause I think they're going to fire him at Aurora B. Scout's honour, Skeeter, I am not passing time with Lamar Del Ray."

It felt almost as if she was pleading with me. Aunt Jenn playing defence was not something you met up with very often.

I took one more chance; it seemed to be my day for it: "Can I see Marty Raymond again? With Zal and CC?"

If I wasn't going to be Nick Storm, I didn't see why Zal and CC should have all the fun. This was the closest I'd ever gotten to a real adventure.

Her face darkened. At last she said, "I'll think about it." We crossed the parking lot. "Straight goods, Skeeter: How'd you pull off skipping school?"

"I had a friend call the office early and leave a voice-mail pretending to be you." It didn't seem right to tell the real way, in case I needed to use it again.

"Fair enough," she nodded. "Always keep it simple. You ever try it again, mind, especially at Studies Institute, I'll have your hide. Skipping school is how I came to be driving a delivery truck."

"It was not," I said. "It was breaking rules."

"Rules are made to be— Wait a minute, smart guy. Isn't skipping school breaking rules?"

She had me there. "*Bad* rules are made to be broken," she went on. "*No skipping* is not a bad rule. We're not paying a king's ransom for you to cut class. The road to perdition starts right there."

"What's perdition?"

"You're the smart one. Look it up."

Up in the apartment, I looked up *perdition*. You can too, if you're interested.

Aunt Jenn showered and rediscovered her open beer. Then, towel around her head, she said, "Now tell me, as I figure out dinner, what was it like wading in there to catch a gator?"

"Caiman," I corrected. "It was scary but kind of fun."

"I know the combination," Aunt Jenn nodded. "All too well. How'd you do it?"

I started to explain as she got out a pot and a frying pan and put them on the stove. Then she held up a finger to interrupt. "I'm doing my world-famous tuna fried rice. Work for you? Then after supper there's still time to hit the library." She was pouring brown rice into the saucepan before I could react. I probably don't need to tell you the rest.

CHAPTER

Big Money Bounce

I think Aunt Jenn worried about me so much because technically I'm an orphan. My parents died when I was six months old, so I don't remember them. I know we lived up north near Gram and Grandpa and that they got in a snowmobile accident. Aunt Jenn was in Nashville then, with her music friends. Before that, she'd travelled all over the world. She came back and got made my guardian. Then she got a job at B&G Trust and transferred here as soon as she could.

Aunt Jenn had pictures of my parents, Katy and Bill. One is of Katy holding baby me. I look like a baby. Katy is pretty and blond and she looks like what she was: Aunt Jenn's younger sister. She was only twenty when she had me.

There was only one picture of Bill. You can't see much of him. He's grinning beside an ice-fishing hut, all bundled up in snow pants and a parka, with the fur-trimmed hood up over his tuque and a big pair of sunglasses against the glare. Bill was from the east coast. He'd gone north to work. Aunt Jenn said he was an only child raised by his grandparents after his fisherperson parents had been lost at sea, and now his grandparents had passed too.

"The one time I met him," Aunt Jenn said, "I was up from Nashville at the time. He told me he'd come north to find his Fortune. And he had, in your mom. That's why he wanted you to have her last name."

"What was his?" I asked.

"Smith. Or was it Jones? Isn't that awful of me? Skeeter, it's been a century."

I've daydreamed about Bill Smith-Jones and Katy. Sometimes we'd be shipwrecked, sometimes lost in the Arctic. Sometimes they'd get tangled up in the stories Aunt Jenn told about herself and her friends: taking a train to the wrong country in Europe, living in the haunted farmhouse with no running water, driving around in the psychedelic pickup truck with the kitchen sinkaphone mounted on the hood, singing backup in a band that almost opened once for the Rolling Stones.

I hadn't thought much about them for a while, though when Studies Institute came up, I had kind of wished we'd suddenly learn that Bill Smith-Jones had left me a fortune his fisher parents had found in a shipwreck long ago.

I'd also wondered about a Nick Storm mystery about an orphan who turns out to be a missing heir, but since Gram worked in a dentist's office and Grandpa was laid off at the mine again, it wasn't going to be me. There'd been too much to imagine and I'd given up. Life with Aunt Jenn was the only life I knew and I liked it, even if there hadn't been much mystery.

Now that life felt a little shaky: I had more mysteries than it was probably healthy to have. Was Aunt Jenn lying about Lamar Del Ray? What flipped her out about Marty Raymond? And how could we catch the Borsalino Bandit?

The day after school got out, CC went to summer camp up north for a week. I biked over to Zal's house to talk about the Bandit.

"Have something for me when I get back," CC had ordered. Secretly, I hoped we'd solve the whole thing before then, just to show her.

Zal was cutting the lawn when I arrived, something I also had to do for Wiley Kendall. While I waited, I goofed around with my own new bouncy ball, a green one with purple swirls. They had them in the plaza variety now.

When Zal finished, we got lemonade and sat in the cool of the garage, with its smells of gasoline and cut grass from the still-ticking lawn mower. No one could overhear us there.

Zal had done his research but there still wasn't much to overhear. The Borsalino Bandit had struck at least nine times that the police could identify. We had the dates for all the robberies. The most recent was the day we caught the caiman. He'd hit different banks: First Savings, Fidelity, Guaranty Mutual, B&G, and all more than once, though never the same branch twice. He was white, medium everything, had a beard, a belly, and wore hats that hid his face from security cameras. A linked story on the Internet said that local sales of men's wide-brimmed summer hats had gone up thirty per cent thanks to talk about them and the Bandit.

Exactly what he did when he robbed a bank, the cops weren't saying. "Afraid of copycats making things more difficult," Zal explained.

Still, he'd found a news item from one of the first robberies that said the robber hadn't shown a gun or anything, just passed a note to a teller demanding money. That didn't make sense to us.

"Why would you hand over money if you didn't have to?" I wondered.

"Ask your aunt," Zal reminded me. "She'll know."

"I will tonight," I promised. "We're coming to your game." Aunt Jenn and I always went to a few of Zal's ball games.

"Cool," Zal said. "It would be pretty sweet if we caught this guy." He squinted at me. "Hey, look at that." He reached behind my ear and held up a dime. "You should wash your hair more often." He stuffed the dime in his pocket.

I couldn't help touching my head. "How'd you do that?"

"It's magic." Then he sighed. "I wish it was. If I could really pull money out of the air we wouldn't need that reward to help pay for school. I think my parents are pretty worried about how much it costs. I might not be able to go. And I really want to go, Dunc. Dang, SI would be so cool."

I was surprised. I looked around me. The garage looked almost bigger than our apartment. Zal's family worried about money? I said, "Aunt Jenn's worried too. She's working like crazy."

Zal sighed again. "You know, Arturo Rocinante makes our fees for Studies Institute every at-bat." He brightened. "Hey, wanta throw a few this aft?"

"Okay," I said. "And then go to the library. I have to cut grass for Wiley Kendall first, though. Call for me after lunch."

Business Bounce

When Zal came by, I put away volume seven of *World's Best* and got my glove. It looked pretty shabby next to his new Arturo Rocinante model. Lots of teachers' cars were still in the parking lot when we got to the ball field at Park Lawn. Miss Linton's yellow Mustang was in the middle.

"Weird to think we won't be back there," said Zal, sounding confident again.

"We will next week." Every summer we all went to the city day camp at Park Lawn. This year we were old enough to be CITs — counsellors in training — and we'd only go half days.

"That's not the same," Zal said. He was right.

We were leaning our bikes against the chain-link

backstop behind home plate when we saw the Gator Aid SUV. It was parked in the driveway of the first house after the apartments ended. Marty Raymond came around the corner of the house and knocked on the door. When no one answered, he turned and saw us, then waved and strolled over.

He was in full Gator Aid glory: boots, cargo pants, safari shirt over his beer belly, and his straw hat. A pair of wraparound shades hung from a little bungee cord around his neck, below the shell on a string. He grinned at us and tipped a finger off his hat brim. "Pardners, we meet again."

I'd stayed away since the blow-up with Aunt Jenn, waiting for her to "think about it." Obviously, Marty Raymond knew what was what because he didn't put me on the spot. Instead, he said, "Zal, right? Much obliged for sending along that video clip; primo footage. Got it running on continuous loop in the store, right beside Chester. Think he likes it. Didn't see you at the grand opening, to say thanks."

Zal nodded and punched the pocket of his glove. "That's okay. I couldn't be there. I got grounded for skipping school that day."

"Uh-oh," Marty Raymond sighed. "Beg pardon, fellas. I guess there was a little fallout from that caper." He looked at me. I didn't know what to say. Marty Raymond went on, "What about your gal pal there? JC?"

"CC. She got grounded too," Zal said. "Her dad said if she'd just told him, he'd have come with us."

"Hey," Marty Raymond crossed his arms over his chest. "My kind of dad." He paused and scuffed at the dirt with a boot toe. Then he looked up and squinted at us from under the hat brim. "Don't suppose I could interest you in a little HRR just now?"

"HRR?" I said.

"Herpetological Rescue and Release. One of Gator Aid's ana-cilliari services."

"You mean *ancillary*?" That was Zal.

"My bad. That is precisely what I mean. Got a lady 'cross the way there, called in a flap. Says there's a snake big as a firehose in the house."

As Zal took a step back and said, "I don't like snakes," I said, "I'm in." Marty Raymond grinned.

"Come on, Zal," I said, "it'll be cool." I had no idea if it would be cool or not, but it was like the last time, in the park: a dare I had to take.

Marty Raymond said, "Won't be a biggie, guaranteed. First off, there are no poisonous snakes native to this area. Second, folks see a garter snake, they think it's a python. They have IRF: Irrational Reptile Fear. Snakes are calm critters: don't mess with them and they won't mess with you. Third, I don't really need the *physical* help, unnerstand, you'd be more on the PR end of things. You wear one of my new T-shirts, I introduce you as Gator Aiders and say this is part of your training. You hand me things and look happy while I do the heavy lifting — not that there'll be any."

"T-shirts?" Zal said.

"Green with gold lettering."

Zal gave in. "As long as it doesn't take long." We got our bikes and walked back to the SUV. The T-shirts were in a box in the cluttered back end, along with cloth bags, cages and an assortment of ropes and poles with odd ends.

"I still don't get it," Zal said, pulling on a T-shirt.

Marty Raymond said patiently, "Your business start-up, it's all about image and outreach. That's why we offer ana — call them extra — services. Gets your name around. Example: next week I'm taking some critters, do a show at the school day camp there. You can bet some families will be down to the shop after that."

"Hey, we'll be there," I said. "We're CITs. We get T-shirts for that too."

"I look forward to it. It all helps with the old cash flow, which right now is mucho importanto, let me tell you."

"But isn't Gator Aid a big multinational?" Zal asked. "You said—"

"Indeed we are, pardner, but that don't mean every operation don't have to pull its weight and more. Let me tell you, I have been doing some major fundraising the last while."

"How?" I asked.

"Let's just say non-traditional ways. Look happy pardners, here she is now."

Black Mamba Bounce

A very pregnant lady was walking toward the house, pushing a stroller with a small child in it. Marty stepped forward.

"Ms. Khalid? Marty Raymond. Gator Aid." They shook hands. "These are two of my Gator Aiders, Zal and Duncan. You might have seen 'em on TV at the caiman rescue."

"Thank you for waiting," Ms. Khalid said. "I just couldn't stand to be in there any longer, with a child, and me like this."

"No worries. The GIs and I will have you fixed up in no time."

"It would be GAs," Zal pointed out.

"Beg pardon. Now just where did you spot the critter, ma'am? Lend a hand there, men." We helped

Ms. Khalid lift the stroller onto the front porch. She unlocked the door.

"In the clothes dryer," Ms. Khalid shuddered. "I had a last load because the backyard line is full and I looked in and there it was, all curled up. It was huge! I screamed and slammed the door and Steven started crying and I just got us out of there as fast as I could and called you on my cellphone. We've been walking ever since."

"You did the right thing," Marty soothed. "Now we will. You can wait out here if you'd rather. Which way's the laundry?"

"Thank you," Ms. Khalid said. "Through the kitchen, down the stairs. Aren't you taking any equipment with you?"

"Just a preliminary assessment. We'll git 'er done. C'mon, men."

Marty Raymond strode inside. Zal and I followed cautiously. The sound of a radio from the kitchen made the silence of the rest of the house more ominous. The screen door's compressor banged it shut behind us.

Zal and I jumped. "I don't like snakes," he said again. "What if the place is infested?"

"Not likely," Marty said over his shoulder. "I scoped the foundation already. It's in good shape, no cracks they'd get in, and there's not a lot of undergrowth next to the walls. Your snake likes that stuff. What there is, though, is a dryer vent about a foot off the ground. A snake looking for shade, or maybe smelling a mouse, is gonna head right in there. They like a confined space." He looked back at us. "Don't worry, guys. I did snake relocations in South Africa for three years. I know my stuff. C'mon."

We followed him through the kitchen and down the basement stairs into the cool.

"What's snake relocation?" I asked

"Farm workers find snakes in fields and orchards and get scared. We'd go out, catch the snakes and release 'em in the wild. Now South Africa, there was a place where your stakes were a little higher."

Did you ever get bitten?"

"Couple times. Scariest was from a black mamba. They're a little dull-grey snake, with only the inside of their mouths black. And that's the part you don't want to see, because they're venomous as all get out. We'd caught one, bagged him, put the bag on the scale to weigh him. I put the catcher pole on him. He was lying flat inside, which usually means they're calm. I went to lift the bag and he struck. Two punctures in my thumb. See?" he showed us his right hand. "Right there; those are the scars. Got me right through the bag. They raced me to the hospital and I could feel myself turning numb: feet, hands slowly shutting down, you know? They shot me full of antivenom serum. That's when it turned out I was allergic to the serum. Anaphylactic shock. It was a fun few days." Marty Raymond chuckled.

"And you still like snakes after that?" Zal muttered.

"Hey, my fault, not the snake's. You'd be pissed too if I stuck you in a bag and weighed you. They're misunderstood, you know? It's my thing, it's in the blood."

It was an unfinished basement. The washer and dryer stood against the far wall, a small window above them. A fluorescent light glared overhead. Marty Raymond turned it off. He bent to the glass of the dryer door, took a small flashlight from a pocket and shone it in.

"Milk snake," he pronounced. "No wonder she's upset. They look like rattlers." He straightened up. "All right, team. Here's what we need: Zal, I know you don't like these critters and I appreciate your hanging in. How about you go on up to the truck please, and get me a snake stick and a hook, both about four footers, and one of the green bags? A stick is one with a handle grip and lever at one end, and jaws at the other. You'll know it. While you're there, tell Ms. Khalid that everything is A-OK, under control, piece of cake, et cetera, not venomous and all but done. You may not like snakes, but I can tell you're a snake charmer. Work a little magic, son."

Meant-to-Be Bounce

Zal zoomed up the stairs. "How'd you know he was a magician?" I said.

"I didn't," Marty Raymond said. "Is he?" I nodded. There was a pause, then Marty Raymond said, "So, Duncan. I guess we're breaking a couple of rules here, dude."

"Yeah." We looked at each other. "You know my Aunt Jenn, huh?"

Marty Raymond nodded slowly. "Sure do. From back in the day."

"How come she doesn't like you?"

"That's between me and her, for now."

"Did you know her from when she did music? Or when she was travelling?"

He hitched his pants and leaned against the dryer.

"Well, I guess she'd a' been doing music. I wasn't part of that. I met her up where your, ah, grandparents lived. They still there?" I nodded. "I tried to get in touch with them a ways back," Marty Raymond said. "But I never heard anything."

"Are you from there?" I asked.

"No. I was just passing through. Met your family."

"Did you know my mom and dad too?" The question just popped out.

"Ah." He cleared his throat and stuffed his hands in his pockets. "Yup. I did, that. Not for long, though. Just passing, like I said."

"Did they like you?"

"I like to think so."

"Was my dad's name Smith or Jones?"

His forehead wrinkled. "Wha—? Oh, um, Smith. Yeah, Smith." He nodded but didn't look too sure. "It was a long time ago." He shifted his weight. "Your aunt says you're a real smart guy, heading to a special school. What do you like doing? More than anything else?"

My mind went blank. "My friend CC would really like all this," I said, to change the subject.

"Yeah, but what about you? What do you like more than anything else?"

"Well, I like writing stuff. Mysteries, I guess. Adventures. Figuring stuff out. I'm reading *The World's Best 100 Detective Stories*. And I'm writing an original story about a jewel robbery that was my idea."

"Far out. A writer. I don't recommend a life of crime. What else are you trying to figure?"

"How come I'm not supposed to see you?" It just popped out.

Marty Raymond scratched his beard, crossed his arms, squinted at me, looked away, then squinted at me again. "You know how I said snakes are misunderstood? Well, I think maybe your Aunt Jenn misunderstands me. Which is understandable. Though I don't think of myself as a snake."

He came off the dryer and started to pace around. "Some stuff is meant to be, Duncan. I ran across the store space in that plaza because, well, I was looking for . . . your Aunt Jenn . . . and she — you — happened to live here. The store is perfect for Gator Aid. And I run into you and your friends because you're looking for adventure, right? *The Mystery of the Gator in Green Pond*, there's one for you."

I wasn't sure that was exactly right, especially since we'd already bombed his SUV with a bouncy ball, but this didn't seem to be the time. Besides, Marty Raymond was on a roll, arms waving. He stepped over a litter of toy building blocks. "See? It fits together. It was meant to be."

Zal came thumping back down the stairs, carrying sticks and one of the canvas bags. "Got everything," he said.

Marty Raymond was still rolling. "That's why I had to wait till now to do Gator Aid. It had to be here." He stopped, seeing Zal. "Of course, Gator Aid International has been running for years. Okay, pardner, what we got?" Zal showed him what he'd brought. "Just what the doctor ordered. How's our client?"

"She hopes we won't be much longer."

"Just long enough so's it seems harder than it is." Marty Raymond winked. He turned the overhead light back on, then handed me the canvas bag and took the stick with the jaws and squeezy handle for himself. Zal kept the one with the hook.

"This'll be good training for you. Our little buddy feels pretty cozy in there. I don't think he'll budge, so here's the drill, compadres." Marty Raymond explained how things would work.

As he talked, he squeezed the levered pistol handle of the snake stick and the rubber jaws at the other end opened. Zal did not look happy. I wasn't sure how I felt, except I figured Marty Raymond could handle it — as long as I didn't think about him dropping the caiman.

"Remember, PCC: patience, calm, control. He's not venomous but if he gets riled he'll still bite, and it hurts plenty. Ready? Let's go," Marty Raymond said.

I reached around from the side of the dryer and pulled the door open as gently as I could. "Hey there, buddy," Marty Raymond said softly, slipping the snake stick inside. "There we go."

I watched his hand ease up on the lever. Gently he withdrew the stick, with the end clamped to the milk snake, just behind the head. It was grey-brown, and big, maybe four feet, with red mottles on its back and black-and-white checks on its stomach. It even made a kind of rattling noise. I could see why Ms. Khalid had been scared. Truth to tell, I was a little scared.

"Hook under him, about halfway back." Zal scooped up the drooping snake as well. "Open the bag."

I dropped the bag on the floor and held it open. I winced as Marty Raymond slid the snake headfirst, past my hands, deep into the bag and squeezed the catcher handle to release it. The tail slipped off Zal's hook and disappeared inside as well.

"Pull the drawstrings." I pulled, fast. Marty Raymond cinched the metal toggle down and laid the snake catcher on the bag. We all stepped back and watched ripples on the canvas as the snake moved.

"Duncan, Zal, primo job. Give him a moment to settle," Marty Raymond said. Zal and I both let out our breath and looked at each other, then at the bag. The snake was still moving.

"Why didn't you come here looking before?" I asked as we waited. "We've lived here a long time. You could have done Gator Aid ages ago."

Marty Raymond coughed and kept his eyes on the bag. After a second he looked at us. "I was doing time."

"You were in *jail*? What for?"

"Smuggling."

"Smuggling? You mean, like, drugs?" Zal said breathlessly.

"Reptiles. First it was just odds and ends for my own

collection. You know, a lizard in your jacket lining, frog in your hat." I nodded as if I did that all the time. Marty Raymond went on, "But after South Africa, I started a business, all legal, importing reptiles for zoos and pet stores. Didn't take long to learn which customs agents at the airport would check your shipment and which ones would just stamp the papers and wave you through. If I timed it to get the right agent, I could have papers for two boas, say, but have five in the crate. Extra profit, see?

"But your real money is in the rarities. People always want what they can't get. Take breeds from Australia: Australia won't let them be exported anymore. So I flew down, got a genuine Australian bearded dragon — never mind how — smuggled it back in a tube I checked through as a rolled-up painting. Big score, guys; got me thinking, I was on a roll. Did a few more deals like that, then aimed right for the top: I went to Madagascar, got me a plowshare tortoise to bring in."

"Was that bad too?" I asked.

"Yeah," Marty Raymond sighed. "First, it's against the law to ship them anywhere; they're an endangered species. Second, my import papers said the tortoise was an albino Burmese python. It would have been fine except the customs lady I expected to be on duty was off sick. Her replacement was bored poking through dirty socks and got all excited to see a big snake." He sighed. "Obviously that didn't work out so good. Anyways, I got four years, ended up doing two and a half. While I was in there, I did some thinking. When I got out, I had some things to do. Gator Aid is one of them. The others," he looked at Zal, then me, "well . . . they're in progress."

The bag was still. Marty Raymond stooped and gently hefted it. Zal gathered the tools and I closed the dryer door.

Upstairs, Marty Raymond told Ms. Khalid everything was fine and gave her some advice about protecting her dryer vent. Even though he said this was a Gator Aid community service, she insisted on giving him a fifty-dollar cheque for the Gator Aider Training Program, and Cokes to Zal and me. She was also going to put a cousin who was looking for "some kind of turtle" in touch with the store. "Bring it on," Marty said.

At the SUV, he said, "As soon as there is a Gator Aider Training Program I owe it fifty bucks. In the meantime it's golden PR, a tank of gas — and maybe a turtle. And a snake I can keep for inventory. Think I'll call him Bob. There's nothing like free."

"It wasn't already part of your inventory, was it?" Zal said.

Marty Raymond laughed. "Planting Chester was a one-off and it worked. Scaring people with snakes in their houses is not a business builder. If it were, I'd do it, believe me. Whatever helps. Speaking of which, you guys did, big time." Zal started to peel off his T-shirt. "Keep it," Marty said. "You deserve it."

"Thanks." Zal looked surprised. He swung onto his bike. "C'mon, Dunc. I need to throw a few."

"Okay," I said. "You go. I'll be right there."

Zal headed for the schoolyard. "I better give my shirt back," I said to Marty Raymond.

"Keep it." He winked. "Say I gave it to Zal to pass along to you. Here's another for your gal pal."

I nodded. "So you don't smuggle anymore?" I asked, taking a shirt for CC.

"Duncan, smuggling was like doing snakes. It's not if you get bit, it's *when* you get bit. But I'll tell you true, it wasn't just the money. There's a thrill. Know what I mean?"

I nodded again. I couldn't deny there'd been a little thrill in some of the things I'd done lately. As if he were reading my mind, Marty Raymond said, "I think you do, or you wouldn't be here right now, where you're not supposed to be."

I felt my face turning red. "Now, I promised your Aunt Jenn something," he said. "And so did you."

"She's thinking about it," I said.

"Well, that's progress. So let's not push our luck, pard-ner. I gather I'll see you next week. Till then, let's neither of us get bit again. At the beach, amigo."

"Pardon?"

"Just goofing. Old saying. Back in the day, I say, 'See you at the beach.' You'd say, 'Twelve o'clock' or 'It's been a slice.'"

"Got it," I said. "It's been a slice." Of what, I wasn't sure.

Third Base Bounce

Aunt Jenn got home on time for once. She frowned hard at my new T-shirt. "Zal got it for me," I said, and we moved on to other things. We had a picnic supper ready for Zal's game.

"Wiley Kendall's coming too," she said. "I brought another order home for him. I had to invite him, to be polite."

This had happened before and was not as bad as it sounded. Zal's games were usually fun, partly because Wiley Kendall and Aunt Jenn knew their baseball and how to keep a scorecard. Anyway, I had a job to do.

We settled in the bleachers on the third base side, to be closer to Zal at shortstop, saying hi to Zal's family, who were a couple of rows down. Aunt Jenn shared out egg-and-onion sandwiches and passed me a drink. Wiley

Kendall *ahem*ed and said thanks, then said, "Too bad that Lamar guy didn't bring my order earlier. Duncan and I could've used it."

Aunt Jenn swallowed some sandwich. "Well, I got the impression no one liked him." She shot a look at me. "I don't think he'll be there much longer, anyway."

We all clapped as Zal's team took the field.

"Ah, well, *ahem*, I wouldn't say I didn't *like* him. There was just something, ah, odd about him."

"It takes all kinds." Aunt Jenn shrugged and dug out a pencil as the first batter stepped to the plate.

The first few innings were dull. Nothing came Zal's way, and he was at the bottom of the batting order for his team. When he finally came to bat, he got caught on a called third strike to end the inning.

"You were robbed, Zal!" Aunt Jenn grinned and shouted through the cheering. She and Wiley both marked their cards. I saw my chance.

"You know when I was in that robbery?" I asked, aiming to sound casual. "I've been wondering, how come alarm bells didn't ring and all?"

Aunt Jenn passed me some grapes. "They didn't want to panic anyone, the robber or the customers. No telling what might have happened then."

"But if the robber just hands you a note? If there's no gun or anything . . ."

"You don't know that. They trained us at the bank: try to stay calm, do just exactly what they tell you. Wait till they leave. It's safer if no one plays the hero."

"Just let the guy get away?"

"Would gunplay or hostages or whatever be better? Think about it, Skeets. That's why I was so worried when you said you hugged that bandit."

"Plus, I think I hurt him," I said. "He was all bent over."

"Maybe," Aunt Jenn nodded. "But he probably ducked on purpose, so he couldn't be measured. There are height strips in bank doorways. Take a look next time." She reached for her soda. "Anyway, the most we might do was try to slip in a dye pack."

"What's that?"

"A paint capsule, pressurized. It breaks and splatters the money. The stains show it's stolen. But some robbers watch for those, so you don't do it if they're on the ball."

"That Borsa-whatsit fella must be pretty on the ball," Wiley Kendall put in.

"Guess so." Aunt Jenn popped a grape in her mouth.

"He's gone a long time without being caught. I could use his money."

"Oh, Wiley, you own our building. We could *all* use the money."

I looked at Wiley Kendall. I hadn't known he owned the eight-plex.

"Speaking of on the ball," Aunt Jenn nodded at the field. *"C'mon, pitcher, atta guy atta guy smoke him!"*

The pitch flew, the aluminum bat pinged and the other team had a man on first.

"*Suck it up,*" Aunt Jenn and Wiley Kendall called, marking their cards. "*Atta boy, keep it low, lookin' to second, atta boy!*"

The pitch flew. The batter lined a shot at Zal, who took it on one hop, flipped it to second and they turned the double play. People clapped. Zal pushed up his glasses and punched the pocket of his Arturo Rocinante glove.

"*Atta go, Zal!*" Aunt Jenn yelled. "His hands get better all the time."

At the end of the game, we all went with Zal and his family for ice cream. Wiley Kendall treated Aunt Jenn and me. "Sweet double play," I said to Zal.

"Thanks," he said. "But I struck out three times."

"You can't have everything." I leaned closer. "I got the bank robbery info."

Zal nodded. "And I got an idea. I can't tell you yet, 'cause I'm not done, but I don't think I'm going to strike out."

CHAPTER

Beach Bounce

"**S**o, what have you got?" CC was back from camp. She'd brought gimp bracelets for each of us, an archery award and a snake-catcher stick she'd made in forest craft class. It was a length of plastic pipe and a knotted rope.

She'd already taken it to show Marty Raymond, who'd said she could use it in his Gator Aid presentation at day camp. That was going to be this afternoon. We were wearing our Gator Aid shirts for his visit. Right now, she, Zal and I, CITs all, were having lunch at Park Lawn, in the shade of an apple tree. It was hot-dog day, a good thing, because I was already sick of the baloney sandwiches I made for myself every morning.

I went first. I told them how the Bandit probably

operated and what would happen in the bank when he robbed it.

"No gun, huh? So maybe we could grab him ourselves. With a net or something. I should have made a giant-size snake catcher."

"Right. If we knew where and when he was going to strike."

"What have you got, Zal?" CC turned to him.

Zal had been looking impatient. Now he said, "I might have cracked the case. I have a theory, anyway. What I can't do yet is prove it."

"Really?" CC hissed. You could tell she wanted to be the case cracker. Truth to tell, *I* wanted to be the one to crack the case. I hadn't gotten anywhere with the other mysteries and this had been my idea.

Zal leaned in. "I think the Bandit could be Marty Raymond."

CC exploded first. "That's the dumbest thing I ever heard! Somebody throw a beanball at you, Zal?"

"Yeah!" I echoed. I almost said, meanly, "Just 'cause you're scared of snakes."

Zal calmly shook his head. "Listen. First, he matches the description: medium build, soft in the middle, dark beard, wide-brimmed hat."

"So what?" I scoffed. "There are tons of guys who look like that."

"You don't rob a bank looking like yourself," CC crowed. "You wear a disguise."

Zal shook his head again. "A smart crook knows everyone will think he's in disguise. But what if he isn't? He can hide in plain sight and no one will suspect. It's the oldest trick in the book."

In fact, it was a trick in *World's Best*. I was stunned. Even CC looked impressed. That didn't happen often. Then she frowned. "Gotta say, even though I really like Marty, he doesn't seem that smart to me."

"They never do," Zal said. "That's part of their evil genius." What could we say? "There's lots more," Zal went on. "He's a convicted criminal. I couldn't find it online but he admitted it to us."

"*What?*" from CC.

"For reptile smuggling," I said. "But that's not bank robbery."

"No, but he did a bad crime for money and he told us he needs money, big time."

"But—"

"And he told us he'd been 'fundraising' in ways he wouldn't talk about."

"But—"

"*And* he's been lying to us about Gator Aid. I searched online. There is no Gator Aid International. There's only his website and it's still under construction."

I gave up saying "but."

Zal sat back. "Remember the day we caught the caiman? And how he showed up late? Kind of rushed? The Borsalino Bandit held up a B&G Trust branch not far from Oakwood Park around noon that day. Think about it."

"I still don't believe it," I said. "And, that's not enough to go to the cops with." I tried to sound sure but inside a tiny part of me was wondering, *could he really have done it?*

"You're right," CC said. "We need more evidence. And we need to try and find out where he was when the other robberies happened."

"I've got a list of the dates and places," Zal said, pulling out the sheet of paper I'd seen before. "I think we should watch Marty."

CC said, "I think we should search Gator Aid."

Marty Raymond arrived at Park Lawn just after lunch. He got us to help him set up in the gym, and he put on a good show, with some big snakes, a legless glass lizard, an iguana, a chameleon and a turtle. He showed his snake-catcher sticks and got CC up to show her homemade one.

The little kids I was sitting with loved it, especially when they got to touch some of the snakes. At the end, they all wanted to make their own snake catchers. Marty Raymond asked Zal to video the whole thing with CC's phone. I just sat there, worry coiling in my stomach like, well, a snake.

I didn't want the guy who taught me how to catch gators and say "see you at the beach," the guy who remembered my name, to turn out to be the Borsalino Bandit, no matter how much we needed money for school or how cool it would be to catch him. I told myself Zal was nuts, that there was no real evidence, that if we investigated we'd prove him wrong.

My worry didn't settle down. It slithered over the memory of Aunt Jenn saying stay away, Marty Raymond was trouble, and tightened round his own words: "There's a thrill, you know what I mean."

After the presentation, we helped him load everything up. "Muchas gracias, pardners," he said. "That footage'll look good in the store and on the website, Zal, which I have got to get online by tomorrow. And, CC, sweet work on that stick. If I bought materials, think you could make a few for the store? Nice little item for the kids."

Zal nodded brightly.

"For sure," CC said. "I could come tomorrow afternoon." How could they seem so relaxed? I got out my bouncy ball to hide my nervousness.

"Hey," said Marty Raymond, "a Super Ball. Haven't seen one since I was a kid."

"Bouncy ball," CC corrected.

"Sure, whatever." He took the ball. "Man, these babies can zing." He looked around. "Hey, c'mon with me." He winked at us and cocked his head at the school.

We ducked back inside and up to the senior wing, far from the day camp and caretakers doing their summer cleaning. Lockers lined both sides of the hallway.

"We're not supposed to be here," Zal warned. He had his ball out anyway.

Marty Raymond just grinned. "Ever play wall ball? Most bounces without hitting the floor wins. Wait'll you hear the sound. Fire at will, pardner."

He and Aunt Jenn were right: it was an awesome sound. It should have made the roof come down, but somehow, right then, it wasn't very satisfying at all.

"Man," said Marty Raymond, "that takes me back."

We scooted down the back stairs and out to the parking lot before anyone came to check. He hitched his pants, looked at his watch and whistled. "Whoo, baby, am I running late. Major appointment, Gator Aiders. Things to do."

Zal elbowed CC, who elbowed me. I winced. "It's been a slice, amigos. See you at the beach." Marty Raymond touched his hat brim.

"Twelve o'clock," I called, as he drove off. The SUV was almost as loud as the bouncy balls hitting lockers.

"What's with the beach?" CC asked.

"Cool as a cucumber," Zal said, almost admiringly.

At Mrs. Ludovic's the suppertime news reported a mid-afternoon robbery. Police suspected the Borsalino Bandit.

CHAPTER 18

Bounce Back

I knew Zal had to be wrong. At least, I thought Zal had to be wrong. I *knew* he and CC were the brainers, but that didn't mean they were always right. Why had I gotten us started on this? I should have just stuck with writing a mystery.

Aunt Jenn got home in one of her jazzy moods and cleaned my clock at pinochle. "What's wrong with you, Skeeter? You look lower than a snake's belly."

It was a bad choice of words.

I didn't feel better until bedtime, when I finished reading "The Two Left Shoes" in volume eight of *World's Best*. The detective proved the police sergeant was wrong about a robbery — the Monkey Burglar didn't do it after all.

Then I knew what I had to do: go along with Zal and CC, to prove that they were wrong too.

When we got together at Park Lawn next morning, they were all about how Marty Raymond had rushed off just before the bank robbery the day before.

I didn't argue, just agreed that CC and I would visit Gator Aid that afternoon, Zal not wanting to be in a place filled with snakes. I didn't care if I was breaking Aunt Jenn's rule again, I needed to keep on top of developments.

"I'll say we've come to work on the snake catchers," CC instructed, as we biked down after lunch. "Then you keep him busy while I look around."

"For anything that connects him to the bank robberies . . ."

"Anything strange," CC said, as we parked and locked our bikes. "You can't tell what might be important. Keep *your* eyes open too."

She was right. Again.

A *Now Open* banner was strung between the two fake palm trees in the store window. Underneath was another sign: *Meet the Oakwood Park Gator.*

The door chimed as we pushed it open. Inside, it was warm. Lights glowed in terrariums big and small. In the biggest, complete with pool and a flat rock, was Chester, the caiman from Green Pond.

A stumpy man I'd never seen before was behind the counter. He had a straggly yellow comb-over, and what he lacked in hair, he also lacked in teeth. He squinted at us through thick glasses. "He'p yez?"

"We're here to see Marty," CC said brightly. "He's expecting us."

The man jerked a thumb over his shoulder. "On the blower. He'p y'self."

"Thanks." CC marched past him, through a doorway, as if she owned the place. I followed. It was detective time.

A large room stretched across the back of the store. Close by, Marty Raymond was perched on the corner of a littered desk, talking on the phone. The far wall had a barred window, a regular door and a larger roll-up one — for deliveries, I guessed. Boxes were stacked there. Beyond them, an air mattress and sleeping bag lay on the floor. Then came another open door showing a sink and mirror. The wall next to us had metal shelves with more boxes, a fridge and a little kitchen counter with a microwave, and dishes in the sink. The middle of the room was taken up with a big work table covered with stuff, including a coil of yellow rope and a bundle of plastic tubing.

There were no masks, no guns, no bags marked *Loot*. Things looked good so far.

Marty Raymond winked at us and spoke into the phone. "Yeah, but they get big. Eight or nine feet, hundred and fifty pounds. You good with that? Reticulated python? Even bigger. You'd need to feed a grown one a sixty-pound goat every so often. How old is your son? Uh-huh, same size as the goat, then. Makes you think, don't it? Why does he want these things? . . . Well, I'm not sure 'because it's cool' is a good reason."

Marty Raymond rolled his eyes. CC walked to the work table. I tried to look casual as I looked around for . . . what? I didn't know.

Marty Raymond said, "A *king cobra*? Look, you really want a constrictor, I can get you a ball python for cheap — fifty to eighty bucks. But I'm not recommending it. Why not bring him down, show him some green iguanas, a chameleon. Start small. We'll set him up with a couple terrariums, misters . . ."

I walked out front. A ball game murmured from a portable radio. The old guy was glumly showing an iguana to a muscle-bound guy with sleeve tattoos. A terrarium beside me was labelled *Chameleon*. I looked in and finally spotted it, exactly the colour of the tree bark it was clinging to. There were no robbery notes tucked in the plant leaves. Next door, the label read *Anaconda*. The snake was thick as a firehose. It also had a big lump in its middle. Would CC think it was a stash of stolen money? I moved on. Beside Chester the caiman, a monitor played Zal's video of the capture. Next was Bob, the milk snake from Ms. Khalid's.

It was all weird, but in a normal way. There was nothing to find, because Marty Raymond was innocent. I turned to get CC. Marty Raymond came out behind me, saying, "That's fine. Ask for Marty," and beeped off the phone. "You met Hank?" He nodded at the old guy. "Old buddy in the trade. He runs the shop when I'm doing community outreach. Didn't expect to see you here."

"It's okay," I lied.

"Glad to hear it, Duncan. You gonna help CC? She's just getting started."

"Well, ah, I just wanted to look around first." Dumb. *World's Best* detectives always knew what to say.

"Cool with me. I've got a few minutes. Let me show you around."

"Oh, that's okay, I—" Then I remembered I was supposed to be keeping Marty Raymond busy. I clammed up and followed.

He opened some of the terrariums. The water monitor's back felt dry and pebbly, like a basketball. The python was named Gloria. Her scales felt almost fake, like soft plastic. Her four rows of teeth looked totally real. I didn't touch those. I was glad when Marty Raymond put her away. We turned to the anaconda. I said, "Maybe it's sick. It looks as if it's got something stuck in it."

"Naw, Slim's fine. That lump is a meal he's digesting. It takes a while."

"What does he eat?"

"Frozen rats. Well, I defrost them first."

I was sorry I'd asked. He smiled. "It's all food, not that much different than eating dead cow. Like I said at your

day camp, mostly we fear things 'cause we don't understand them. Look here."

The sign on the terrarium read *Poison Dart Frogs*. It
took a while to spot the little green-and-black frogs under
the plant leaves. Marty Raymond said, "In the Amazon,
native people take the toxin from these critters and smear
it on the tips of their arrows. It's a paralytic, fatal." He
lifted the lid on the terrarium. I stepped back. "But these
guys are actually harmless. The toxin doesn't come from
the frogs. It comes from a kind of ant they eat in the wild."
He took the top off a pill container and shook a couple
of black pellets into the terrarium. "I feed 'em crickets.
No ants, no toxin, no trouble. Environment means a lot."

As we talked, Hank shuffled in and out of the back-
room, piling things on the front counter. CC wouldn't
be liking that, but I was sure there was nothing for her
to find anyway. I started to relax. Marty Raymond said
to the muscle-bound man, "Buying ol' Betty? An iguana
makes a great pet. Affectionate as all get out. Ride your
shoulder, watch TV."

CC came out of the backroom with an armload of
rope and tubing. "I just remembered," she called to Marty Raymond, "I have my harmonica lesson. We can take
this with us and make some at home, okay? I'll bring
them in really soon." CC hustled me out the door.

"Do you really have a harmonica lesson?"

"Trumpet."

"I thought it was saxophone."

"That was before banjo. Anyway, it doesn't matter, it's not till tomorrow. I can't do a good search with the old guy barging in all the time. We'll have to come back when there's only one of them there."

"Sorry," I said. "I couldn't keep them both out. You didn't find anything, did you?"

"Well, no loot or anything, but there was one strange thing. On the desk there was a passport and a plane ticket to Mexico. The picture in the passport looked kinda like Marty but it was hard to tell because there was no beard or moustache."

"So?"

"The name in the passport was different. It said Lamar Del Ray."

Bandits Bounce

"**W**e better get Zal," I said, and took off on my bike. I didn't answer any of the questions CC called at me, just yelled back, "I'll tell you there."

She was steamed by the time we got to Zal's. He was in the garage, flicking cards at a Styrofoam board. When he got it right, they'd stick in like ninja stars. Most were on the concrete floor. "What did you find?" he asked.

"Tell him," I ordered CC.

She scowled at me and told. "I got a picture of the passport," she finished. "It's not very good because the old guy came in just as I was taking it."

She pulled out her phone and showed us. CC was right. Her hand holding the passport open had gotten in the way as she tried to show two pages at once. Most of the photo was chopped off: from the nose down, it could have been a clean-shaven, short-haired Marty, or not.

"Lamar Del Ray," Zal said slowly. "I know that name from somewhere."

I shook my head. "Doubt it. He's a guy who works at Aurora B with my Aunt Jenn. He has a beard and moustache too. That picture might be either one of them, shaved."

"The picture looked like Marty," CC insisted. "Sort of. I only got a glimpse."

Zal said, "So Marty Raymond either has this Lamar guy's passport or a fake one with his own picture in it. But why? What's it got to do with the Bandit?"

I sighed. "I don't know, but I can tell you this much. My Aunt Jenn knows Marty from way back. She says he's trouble, and I'm not supposed to see him. I don't know the connection to Lamar Del Ray. I only met him once, when he delivered to our building. I didn't like him. Aunt Jenn said she felt sorry for him."

I leaned in close. "But here's the thing: Remember you said how Marty Raymond showed up late the day we caught the caiman? And there was a bank robbery right before? Well, I saw Lamar Del Ray the same day. He zoomed into the park in Aunt Jenn's car, and later I saw Aunt Jenn driving it out of the park. She said he borrowed it for a job interview. But what if he didn't go for a job interview? What if . . ."

"He robbed a bank," CC finished for me. "And met Marty. Or Marty handed off to him. He's got a beard and moustache?"

I nodded. "And he has, like, a leather cowboy hat. Wide brim."

Zal whistled. "The Bandit Brothers."

"The Twin Thieves," CC put in. "No, the Thief Twins."

"They don't look *that* much alike," I corrected. I had kind of hoped telling about Lamar Del Ray would somehow help to clear Marty Raymond.

"Either way," Zal said, "we have another suspect. We have to find out about this guy and how he connects to Gator Aid. Does your Aunt Jenn know where he lives?"

I shrugged. "She gave him a lift partway home once."

"You *guys*," CC snorted. "That's why I tried to photograph two pages of the passport. The other has an address."

We huddled over her phone. CC fiddled with it. "Three sixteen Pacific Avenue," Zal read out. A quick check told us it was the other side of Oakwood Park. We got permission to go ride the Trails. We told ourselves that straying a block or two past the other side wasn't going to make much difference.

"What'll we do if he's there?" I wondered as we pedalled.

"Nothing yet," said CC. "We just need to know where

he is so we can tail him if we have to. If he's not, maybe we could search the place."

"*What?*"

"Can't you guys ride any faster?"

CHAPTER

Aurora B Bounce

The address was a tall, skinny old house on a street of tall, skinny old houses, crowded with locked bikes, recycling bins and parked cars. A wire fence marked off a scraggly patch of grass and weeds. A hand-lettered sign, *Rentals Available*, curled on itself in the blank picture window. Junk mail overflowed three letter boxes. I imagined Wiley Kendall shaking his head.

The gate creaked as CC unlatched it. We crowded up the cracked concrete walkway.

"What *will* we do if he's here?" Zal repeated my question.

The only answer he got was a long, low growl. A big black dog stalked around the corner of the house, ears back, hackles up. I felt the hairs on my own neck prickle the same way.

I don't know what kind of dog it was, but it seemed just smaller than a horse. It growled again, deep in its throat, then gave a thunderclap bark and took a step toward us. I took a step back.

"Freeze," CC said to us. "Stand straight. And don't make eye contact. I'm on this."

We froze. "Hey fella," CC said in a soothing voice. "How are you, big guy?" She reached in her pocket. The dog took another step, still growling. He barked again and I flinched. CC's voice went on, "I bet you could use a little snack, couldn't you?"

"Don't give him ideas," Zal croaked.

"Shut up. Look away. What do you say, fella, a little treat go good now? Huh?"

I heard the dog's collar clink as he came closer, still growling. I looked up at the saggy line of the porch roof and tried to hold still. It was tough, let me tell you.

"You could chew on Dunc or Zal, but I bet you'll like these better," CC coaxed. More growls. Something pattered to the ground. There was snuffling, then an unpleasant crunching. I risked a look. The dog swallowed. He looked expectantly at CC. His ears had come forward and his neck hairs were down.

"Sure, I've got another," she said. "I told you you'd like them. Those guys are too skinny anyway."

She held out something. The dog gobbled it down. "Stay still till he gives us the sniff test," CC said quietly. "Then we're good."

There was a lot of steam-engine panting as the dog circled us. "That's my boy," CC said. "You're just a big pussycat, aren't you? Can you sit for me? Sit."

As she talked, the front door of the house jerked open. A stout lady in pink shorts stepped out. The dog bounded over. "What's all this? Whaddya want?"

"We were just saying hi to your dog, ma'am," CC said brightly.

"What? Spig up." Somewhere inside the house a TV was blaring.

"JUST SAYING HI TO YOUR DOG," Zal bellowed, probably in relief. The dog wheeled and started to bark.

"Shut up, Zal," hissed CC.

"Shut up, Rex," said the stout lady.

"Actually, ma'am," CC walked to the porch, "we were looking for a friend of ours who lives here. Lamar Del Ray?"

"What? Who?"

"Lamar Del Ray. We thought he lived here."

"No Monterey here. Never has been. Last tenant was a Murray." The stout lady jerked her head at the empty window. Her yellow hair was in curlers.

"Really?" CC stepped up on the porch. "My drum teacher is named Murray."

"Different Murray. Wasn't a gym teacher. Worked in a pet shop. Anyway that was a month back. Long gone. And didn't pay his hydro, neither."

"Well, sorry to disturb you," CC said. "Guess we got

it wrong. Nice meeting you, Rex." She patted the dog's head and slipped him another something.

Rex trotted after us to the fence. It wasn't until CC fastened the gate behind us that Zal and I let out our breath. We got our bikes. CC tossed something to Rex. Gobble, gobble, gobble. "What is that stuff?" I said to her as we got on our bikes.

"Doggie treats."

"Why do you have a pocketful of doggie treats?"

"For times like this." CC shrugged. "Doesn't everybody?"

Zal saved me answering. "That was useless," he sighed, pushing off on his bike. "And ridiculously scary."

"Says you," CC sniffed, keeping up. "I got a look in the window when I was on the porch. The only thing in the room was a cowboy hat. We were on the right trail, just too late."

I could only think of one thing to do. We talked over the how-to, then CC handed me her phone. My hands shook a little as I punched in the number for Aurora B. I crossed my fingers that Aunt Jenn wouldn't answer. She didn't.

"Is Lamar Del Ray there, please?" I went for a Wiley Kendall kind of voice.

"Who?"

"Lamar Del Ray. Is he on today?"

"Lamar Del— Hang on, I'll check." I heard muffled voices, then, "Sorry, no one here by that name."

"Oh. Well, I just need to check his address. Will he be in tomorrow?"

"Nope. Far as I know, never had anyone by that name working here. Can someone else help?"

"No, that's okay. Thanks." I clicked off. I handed CC her phone back and told the others. We had another mystery on our hands.

As if we needed more complications, Zal said thoughtfully, "That lady back there didn't hear very well. What if 'Murray' was really 'Marty'?"

CHAPTER 21

Bye-Bye Bounce

"**D**uncan, I'm worried about your Aunt Jenn." Wiley Kendall had me cornered as he helped me gas up the lawn mower the next afternoon. It was favourite-chat time again.

"She's okay. Do I keep pouring?" The gas container was heavy.

"Keep it coming. She's working too much, Duncan. All the time. She's moody. I think she's losing weight."

"She says it helps her keep her girlish figure."

"Her figure's always . . . sensational." Wiley Kendall's face got red and he busied himself screwing the cap back on to the gas tank.

I changed the subject. Fast. "Do we start the lawn mower now?"

"Put the nozzle back in the container and cap it. How much this SI school cost?"

"Twenty-five thousand dollars."

"*Twenty*— A *year*? It better be a darn good school. And don't you let her down."

I pressed the priming button three times, then yanked hard on the cord. The motor caught, barely. Wiley Kendall watched me cut the first couple of passes. I was glad when he left, and of the lawn mower's racket. It meant I didn't have to talk to anybody.

Things were definitely not going as planned: Marty Raymond a Borsalino Bandit suspect; Aunt Jenn saying he was bad; and now Lamar Del Ray was in it. Somehow. At least he was a suspect I preferred but, like I said, a whole other mystery himself, and maybe the key to the whole thing.

My only lead was whatever Aunt Jenn knew, and that just made things worse. Finding out was tricky because I couldn't let on I was trying to find out.

The night before, I'd waited until she'd poured an iced tea, then looked up from *World's Best* and asked, as if I'd just thought of it, "Oh, hey, we were biking this aft and I thought I saw Lamar Del Ray. Where does he live? Remember you gave him a lift home one time?"

"Only partway, hon." She turned to put the pitcher of tea back in the fridge. "Where were you?"

"By Oakwood Park."

"Well, I dropped him over to Glendale Mall that time. That's the other direction." Aunt Jenn sipped her tea. "Though he wasn't working today. He's only part-time."

"He didn't get the job he applied for?"

Aunt Jenn looked blank for a moment.

"When you loaned him the car?" I reminded.

"Oh. Right. Guess not. Or maybe . . . I think it was only part-time too."

What? So why did Aurora B Nurseries say they'd never heard of Lamar Del Ray? Did whoever I'd talked to not know all the part-timers? Or was Aunt Jenn lying? And if she was lying, why? I didn't even want to think about that. I thought instead about my own lies to her. Did this run in families? That was another question.

There were so many questions now I couldn't keep track of them all, let alone give them answers. *World's Best* mysteries weren't like this. They were puzzles that unfolded neatly. I didn't feel like the smart detective. I felt like the bumbling cop.

As I cut the parking-lot edge of the lawn, CC rode up and started yelling. I let go of the throttle, and in the sudden quiet I heard, "—gone. That Hank guy says—"

"What? Who's gone?"

"Marty Raymond is gone. That Hank guy wouldn't say where. Didn't know when he'd be back, either. Just said it was business. I'll call Zal. Come to my place soon as you're done."

B&G Bounce

CC, Zal and her dog Roxy were sitting in her family's bass boat when I got there. The boat was on a trailer parked in the driveway, beside their RV. CC had put the canopy up for shade. Roxy barked a hello. I climbed in and CC opened a cooler and handed me a freezie. I needed one.

She'd already told Zal her news. I told what I'd found about Lamar Del Ray. "Maybe he lives over by Glendale now," I finished.

"I wonder if he ever lived on Pacific," Zal said. "Or if Marty Raymond did. And I wonder where Marty lives now." He shifted in his trolling seat. Roxy put her head in his lap. Roxy was a big golden Lab, and gentle as all get out. Zal patted her but he looked comfortable as a worm on a hook.

"I think Marty lives in back of Gator Aid. There was a sleeping bag and air mattress and stuff there," CC said, slurping her freezie.

She tugged Roxy back into the shade and the dog flopped down. CC's shoes were off. Her snake stick was beside her. I crunched some ice, remembering the back-room of the store.

"Hmm," Zal nodded. "I found some things too." He left us hanging while he methodically rolled up the freezie sleeve to the bottom of what was left. CC groaned. Zal ignored her. "I said I knew Lamar Del Ray's name? I remembered from where. I did a search on reptile smuggling after we were at Ms. Khalid's. I didn't find Marty's case, but there was a news story from four years ago about this guy who got arrested at the border with fifty turtles in his sweatpants. Guess what his name was?"

"Lamar Del Ray," cried CC. "He's a reptile smuggler too! I bet they've gone smuggling together."

"There's a way we might find out," Zal said. "Is the Gator Aid number in your phone?"

CC called it up and passed the phone to Zal.

"Should have thought of this before," he said, as he waited for an answer. I thought about what it would be like to have fifty turtles in your pants. Zal said into the phone, "Hi, is that Hank? Just wondering if Lamar Del Ray is there . . . Oh, okay. Thanks. Bye."

Zal looked at us. "He said he'll be back in a few days."

"They *have* gone smuggling," CC gasped.

"Or gone to rob someplace else."

"Or taken off for good with the bank robbery loot," Zal added. "Maybe they were partners. Maybe they took turns being the Bandit. I wonder if Marty's sleeping bag is gone."

"Wait," I said. "They can't be smugglers *and* bank robbers. Marty Raymond will be back. He knows all about snakes and reptiles and he told me Gator Aid is his dream. I know he's been a smuggler, but I don't think he knows anything about bank robbery."

"You're just saying that 'cause you like him." CC crumpled her freezie sleeve.

"Sure I like him," I admitted. "But it's not just that. I mean, would you really not disguise yourself to rob a bank?"

"I already explained that," Zal sighed. He'd finished his freezie. He put the neatly rolled up sleeve in his pocket, took out a quarter and began to practise walking it across his fingers again.

I tried again. "It's not just that. I've been thinking. I rammed into the Bandit's gut, right? It was pretty soft. Marty Raymond's got a big gut, but it looks too hard. You know?"

I was lying again. I hadn't been thinking about guts at all. It was just the first thing that popped into my head to continue the argument.

"What about Lamar Del Ray?"

"I dunno. He's got a big gut too."

"So," Zal said, still walking his quarter, "you're saying that if you rammed them both in the gut you could make a positive ID?"

"Well, no. I just mean that maybe we shouldn't rush into—"

"Listen," CC interrupted, "I like Marty too. He may not be the sharpest knife in the drawer, but I like him." She lifted her snake stick like a sword. "But if he's a bank robber, I want to catch him and I want some of that reward. I could get a kayak and new fishing gear and—"

It was quite a list. CC's family was not going to have trouble paying for Studies Institute. "And we'd be famous," she finished, waving the stick. "Hey, maybe he's hiding the loot in his snake sticks!"

"That's my idea," I reminded her. I'd almost forgotten I'd told her my mystery plot. I sighed. "Look, what else have we got? There has to be something else."

Zal pulled a familiar paper from his pocket and flattened it out. "We've been over this all before. Here's the list of robberies."

"That's done," said CC. "What we need to do is search Gator Aid. And I bet old Hank knows more than he's telling. He's gotta be smarter than he lets on."

She and Zal started talking about how to do it.

I took the paper from Zal and looked at the list of banks and dates for the millionth time. Maybe it was because I wanted to be smarter than I let on too, or maybe it was just dumb luck, but this time, I saw something.

"Hey," I interrupted, "listen."

I went slowly, talking it through to myself as much as them. There was no way I wanted to get this wrong. "The Borsalino Bandit has robbed eleven banks, right? He's hit all different ones, at different times and in different parts of the city, sometimes two different branches of the same bank in a row. The time between robberies changes all the time."

"Old news, Dunc." CC looped her snake stick over a big toe and pulled it tight.

"I know, but look at this." I flattened the sheet across my knees and pointed. "Banks three, six and nine were B&G Trust, and the branches were in the east, north and south ends of town. That could be a pattern. And if it is, it means the twelfth robbery—"

"Isgoingtobehereinthewestendandit'sgoingtobe-aB&G." CC shouted.

"And there's only two west branches and one of them is down in the plaza," Zal finished, stabbing at the paper with his finger. "Look, I've got a list of all the bank branches there too."

I glared at them. I hadn't interrupted all their dramatic stuff. "Right. That means there's a fifty-fifty chance."

"Stakeout," Zal said.

"But my family's going camping this weekend," CC complained.

Zal nodded. "And I've got a ball tournament. But I'll

bet you anything that nothing happens till Marty Raymond gets back. If he comes back."

"He'll come back," I said. "And I'll bet *you* anything that the robber won't be him."

I climbed out of the boat and onto my bike. "It's been a slice. See you at the beach."

CHAPTER

Bandana Bounce

'll admit it wasn't your textbook stakeout, none of us being there all weekend. We wouldn't have been allowed to hang around the plaza all day anyway. (Getting permission from parents was not something *World's Best* detectives had to do.) I myself was busy helping Wiley Kendall. I rode my bike down to the store a couple times, but all I saw was Hank stumping to Donut World for coffee.

It didn't matter. The Bandit didn't strike over the weekend. I'd been half hoping he would, figuring that would somehow prove Marty Raymond was innocent. Monday afternoon, CC went to the store straight from day camp and found Marty was back. She was excited when she told me. She said Marty seemed pretty excited too.

"I'm calling Zal," she announced. "Time to ramp things up."

We met in the cheesy parkette across from the plaza. There was a picnic table, a rusty swing set and a climber. It did have a good view of the parking lot, Gator Aid and B&G Trust.

Weekday stakeout wasn't going to be much easier than weekend, seeing as we all had day camp every morning. Still, we made the best plan we could. From now on, CC would make snake catchers in the store each afternoon, to keep an eye on Marty Raymond. Zal and I would be in the parkette. If a robber drove up, we'd try to flatten his tires, call CC to film him with her phone, and then the cops. I had Sergeant Castro's card in my pocket.

"Anything on Lamar Del Ray?" Zal asked CC.

She shrugged. "Thought Hank said his name, but they were in back, talking low."

We watched all afternoon. *World's Best* stories tended to leave out the waiting bits and cut to the chase. Real-life stakeout was the most boring thing I'd ever done, except maybe for rooting up dandelions with Wiley Kendall, and even that took less time. I wished I'd brought a book, though I guess I couldn't have watched and read at the same time.

Finally, CC said, "Let's blow this pop stand," and we all went home for supper.

The next couple of days weren't any better. CC went in the store. Zal and I took ball gloves and checkers to the parkette. Marty Raymond waved to us when he walked to Donut World.

"It spoils it if he knows we're here," I said.

Zal shook his head. "He doesn't know *why* we're here."

What kept us going was CC said Marty and Hank kept talking about Thursday. And, she told us, she wasn't allowed in the backroom.

"I bet Lamar's hiding there," Zal said. "Or the loot."

"Or a smuggled pterodactyl." I rolled my eyes. I'd had about enough. Wiley Kendall had jobs for me to do. They paid more than this.

"Maybe Hank's the mastermind," said CC, ignoring this, "and Marty and Lamar are his pawns. Either one of them might rob the bank Thursday."

"Or the one we're not staking out. Or not rob anything at all. Listen you guys," I said, "do you really think Marty Raymond is going to rob the bank two doors from his own store? What's he going to do, stroll over when he goes for coffee?"

"Remember about hiding in plain sight?" Zal looked at me. "You said—"

"I know, the oldest trick in the book." I sighed. "But nothing's going to happen Thursday." I wished I knew it for sure.

"Hey," CC said, "it was your idea to catch the Borsalino Bandit. And you predicted it would be here. He hasn't struck anywhere else, has he? You want the reward or not? I say, one more day."

Thursday, no matter how much I told myself nothing would happen, I was still nervous. I didn't even know if I wanted nothing to happen. The day was a scorcher. The parkette was dusty and deserted, the plaza dead. Heat shimmered up from the parking lot. CC texted us that Marty was out somewhere. I didn't know if that was good or bad.

It was too hot for catch, too hot even for checkers. We sat in the shade under the picnic table. I rolled my bouncy ball in the dust and wished I was in the library, where it was air conditioned and never boring.

"It's too hot for this," I said. "Marty Raymond isn't even here."

"He could be robbing the other branch right now," Zal said.

"I bet he's not robbing anything. This is dumb."

"Look." Zal pointed. A bearded guy with a straw hat, sunglasses and a beer gut was slouching across the parking lot toward B&G Trust, carrying a shopping tote. The gut made the egg-white legs poking from his plaid shorts look even skinnier. It wasn't Marty Raymond. Was it Lamar Del Ray? I'd only seen him once full on and once driving by. As I wondered if you'd wear shorts and sandals to rob a bank, he walked into B&G.

We ran to the curb. Zal was already calling CC. As we waited for cars to pass, CC dashed out of Gator Aid, phone ready. Moments passed. There were more cars. Zal and I bounced anxiously at the curb.

The man came out of the bank. CC raised her phone.

A second later, a lady leaned out the door after him. "Vic," she called, "don't forget, extra diapers!" He waved and headed for the supermarket.

CC shrugged and went back inside. Zal and I crossed the street anyway. We needed a freezie. We took our time in the variety store's air conditioning. As Zal checked out the baseball magazines, his ringtone sounded in his pocket.

"Aren't you going to answer that?"

"Nah, it'll be my sister. She calls to bug me. Everyone else texts."

The tone stopped. It started again as we paid for our freezies. Zal sighed and ignored it. We got our change and walked outside.

The next thing we heard was CC, yelling. She ran toward us, waving every which way. "*You guys!* You missed it! You missed it! Why didn't you answer? *GEEZ!* You missed it! It was him, it had to be! Beard, hat, sunglasses. I saw him pull up and head for the bank. He had a little blue backpack. I called *you guys* but *nobody answered.*"

"Was it Marty Raymond?" I interrupted.

"No, but it might have been that Lamar guy and *you* weren't there to see him. All I could do was grab Bob and run out and dump him on the driver's seat before the guy came back."

"Bob the milk snake?" I didn't get it.

"Yes! I thought Bob might scare him enough that he

couldn't get away. But it didn't work. He came out, got in the car and drove off."

"What kind of car was it?" Zal asked.

CC looked disgusted. "I don't know. Small. I only know trucks."

"Did you get a picture? The licence number?"

"No. I put down my phone to grab Bob *when you didn't answer*. The licence was A-W something. Five. I think. I was busy. Unlike some people," she glared.

Zal said calmly, "Do we know the bank got robbed?"

We turned to B&G Trust. It seemed sleepy as ever.

"Remember what my Aunt Jenn said?" I reminded.

A police cruiser whisked up to the bank. Officers strode inside.

"I guess that answers that," CC said.

"What can we tell them?" I sighed.

"Nothing," said CC. "No car, no licence, no video and you're the only one who knows Lamar Del Ray. All I did was lose Bob."

An unmarked cruiser pulled in beside the blue-and-white. Detective Yee and Sergeant Castro went into B&G. CC went to get a freezie.

We ate our freezies in the shade of the plaza canopy, talking about what to do.

"Tell them about Bob," Zal suggested.

We walked to the bank. They weren't letting anyone in. As we stood there, the Gator Aid SUV rumbled up.

Marty Raymond leaned out the window. "Howdy,

Aiders. Hey, why the long faces, as the bartender said to the herd of horses?" Marty Raymond was grinning like a maniac.

"We just messed something up," said CC, staring at him.

"Well I myself, Aiders, just dropped off a friend in a sweet, sweet deal. I'm predicting a genuine game changer." He looked at me and winked. "And to prove it, I'm gonna spring for another freezie, all round."

Some people came out of the bank. A police officer followed them. She started to put yellow crime-scene tape across the door.

"What's that about?" Marty Raymond asked blandly.

"It was just robbed," I said.

"Huh," he said, wiping his face with a blue bandana. "There goes the neighbourhood."

CHAPTER

Butt Out Bounce

Aunt Jenn would have called Marty Raymond higher than a kite, and me lower than a snake's belly. The last one was a good fit, anyway.

"Did you hear him?" CC seethed after Marty had left us outside the variety. "He was practically bragging he did it."

"Except he didn't, did he?" I protested. "You saw the robber wasn't him. And it wasn't the SUV. And why would he give himself away by bragging?" I left the blue bandana out of it.

"I told you he's not the sharpest knife in the drawer, Dunc. So it was that Lamar guy. And he's in on it. They're thick as thieves!"

"They really would be thieves," Zal pointed out.

"*If* it was Lamar Del Ray. All we've got for sure is that they know each other. Well, Lamar knows Aunt Jenn too, and nobody's calling her a bank robber!"

"'Course not," Zal said. "All we've really got is a snake in the getaway car and that really could be important. We could use that reward, Dunc. Try calling that sergeant again."

As usual, he was right. They still weren't letting anyone into the bank, and the cop at the door had told me Sergeant Castro was busy. Zal handed me his phone. This was my third try, which told me Sergeant Castro was not in a mood to be bothered. I went for it anyway.

"Hi, Sergeant Castro, this is Duncan Fortune speaking."

"Yes? What can I do for you, Mr. Fortune? This is a bit of a bad time."

"You told me to call if I thought of something?"

"Help me, Mr. Fortune. Call about what? I'm in the middle of something here."

"I'm the one, the kid, who hugged the bank robber. Remember?"

"Right, right, got it. Duncan. Studies Institute and all that."

"Yes, sir. Maybe you saw me and my friends on the news when we helped capture the caiman in Oakwood Park."

"Missed that, Duncan. You do get around, though.

What's the purpose of your call? As I said, I'm pretty busy this minute."

"Well, we happened to be at the bank robbery this afternoon too?"

"What? Again?"

"We live right near there. We're just outside right now. But we weren't in the bank, just the parking lot, on stake-out, like—"

"Stakeout? That's our job, Duncan."

"I know, but see, we had this theory that the robber would strike there, and anyway, my other friend CC threw a snake into the robber's car, to see if that would scare him, like, and slow him down?" I waited for Sergeant Castro to say something, but he didn't. "But it didn't and he drove off, so we just thought, if you get any reports of cars with snakes in them . . . Because we had an idea who it might be? Just in case of the . . . uh, reward?"

The silence continued.

I was not feeling like Studies Institute material.

Finally, Sergeant Castro said, "What kind of car, Duncan?"

"CC didn't know. She only knows trucks."

"I see. Licence?"

"A-W something. Maybe. And a five."

There was another silence. Then Sergeant Castro said, "Duncan, you're a bright young guy and I'm sure this was a well-intentioned call. You're a mystery fan, right?"

"How did you know?"

"I'm a detective. And as a detective, here's some professional advice: don't meddle in police business. This is not TV or the movies. I've noted your call. Missing pets should be reported to Animal Control. Thank you, Duncan. Goodbye."

CHAPTER

Bob's Bounce

I felt stump toad dumb. I think we all did, because we agreed to be quiet about what we'd done. At dinner, Mrs. Ludovic's TV had coverage of the latest Borsalino Bandit robbery. Sergeant Castro came onscreen. They mentioned the reward again; this time there was a hotline number to call. I wrote the number down, feeling even glummer.

I knew I'd missed my chance. The only good thing was that Marty Raymond hadn't been the bank robber. I didn't know about Lamar Del Ray, but looking back, suspecting Marty Raymond was clearly one of Zal's very few stump toad ideas.

After dinner, I met up with CC and we went to watch Zal's ball game. He didn't make any double plays, but he snagged a wild one-hopper and a liner through the pocket.

"Good fielding," I told him afterward.

"I still struck out three times," he sighed.

"Whatever," CC said. "First time I shot a .22, I couldn't even hit the ground."

"You've shot a gun?" we both said.

"Forget you heard that."

I was home, just finishing "The Murder at Fenhurst" in volume four of *World's Best*, when Aunt Jenn finally got in. I went down to the parking lot to help with groceries. Wiley Kendall helped as well. "That Bandit fella robbed the B&G this afternoon," he told her. "Got clean away."

"That's terrible." Aunt Jenn looked red-faced and tired. "Anybody hurt?"

"No, the news said he always just passes a note, but still. Maybe it's just as well you aren't working there anymore, Jenn, stuff like that happening." I kept my mouth shut. I'd had enough of feeling like a stump toad.

"What is this world coming to?" Aunt Jenn said as we started up the stairs. "My gosh, I'm beat. Glad I shopped this afternoon; I'd have dropped doing it tonight."

I got up for day camp as Aunt Jenn left for work next morning. She said she'd be home to make supper. I was pouring cereal when I heard a scream from the parking lot. I ran to the balcony. Aunt Jenn was scrambling out of her car. She slammed the door behind her. "A snake," she cried. "There's a snake in the car!"

For a second, it was as if she was talking Martian, then it hit me. "Aunt Jenn!" I yelled. "Is it a milk snake?"

"How the hell do I know!" She was waving her hands and backpedalling.

"Don't touch anything!" I called down. "Wait for me!" I dashed inside and grabbed the phone. This time Sergeant Castro would have to listen.

CHAPTER

Better Bounce

By the time I got down the stairs and out into the parking lot, Mrs. Ludovic was following me to see what the fuss was about, and Wiley Kendall was peering in the open window of the car, the big broom in his hand. He reached for the door handle.

"Don't!" I yelled.

He and Aunt Jenn both spun around.

"I just called the police hotline," I panted. "They said not to touch anything. They'll be here as soon as they can. They're checking out other leads."

"Hon," Aunt Jenn said, "what are you talking about? This is either an accident or a dumb joke. I'm sure Wiley could—"

"You don't understand," I said. "This is the bank

robbery car. From yesterday at the plaza. We were there. Lamar Del Ray could be the bank robber! CC dumped a snake in the car to try and stop him."

"How could— I was nowhere near the plaza yesterday," Aunt Jenn yelled. "I went to work and I shopped."

"Someone could've stolen your car," Wiley Kendall said.

"What? While—"

"CC's on her way," I cut in. "She can tell us. She saw the car. If it's yours, I bet Lamar Del Ray stole it. Remember that time you loaned it to him? There was a robbery that day too. The police have to stop him and—" I sucked it up "—maybe Marty Raymond, before they get away. Then we'll get the reward!"

Wiley Kendall's mouth hung open. Mrs. Ludovic exclaimed something I didn't understand. Aunt Jenn swayed and stumbled against the car. Wiley Kendall dropped the broom and caught her.

"Thank you, Wiley," she said faintly. "When will they get here?"

"An hour at least, they said."

Aunt Jenn nodded and shuddered out a breath. "I think I have to go upstairs and sit down. My gosh, what a shock. I do hate a snake, and if somebody stole the car . . ."

"Lamar Del Ray."

Wiley Kendall said, "Isn't he the—"

Aunt Jenn waved her hand in front of her face.

"Whoever. It's too much. Wiley, Dunc, you keep an eye on the car, if that's what they want."

"You better call work, let them know you'll be late," Wiley called after her. We watched Aunt Jenn cross the parking lot, Mrs. Ludovic hustling in her slippers to keep up. "Shock does that," he said. "She'll be okay."

I peered in the open window of the car. Partway under the passenger seat, a milk snake, like the one from Ms. Khalid's, was coiled lazily. I pulled back.

CC rode up a few minutes later, Zal right behind, to meet me for day camp. I filled them in on what had happened.

"Is this the car from yesterday?" I asked CC.

She sized it up. "I *think* so. Little cars all look the same to me. Now a pickup—"

"It's not an A-W licence," Zal pointed out.

CC looked in the car. "But that's Bob all right. Hi, Bob."

"Are you sure it's Bob?"

"Pretty sure. He's a milk snake, anyway. How else would one get in your car?"

"How did one get in Ms. Khalid's house?" Zal asked.

"You 'think so' and you're 'pretty sure'?" I felt a swirl of doubt. What had I gotten myself into now? "We're going to look pretty stupid if you're wrong, C."

"You're the one who called the cops."

We circled the car, peering in for clues I wasn't sure I wanted to find, then helped Wiley Kendall rope off the car with orange traffic cones and gardener's twine.

"Duncan," he said, "I'm going up to check on your aunt."

Zal, CC and I paced the parking lot.

"Well," CC said, "on the bright side, I get Bob — or Bob II — back to Marty. Wonder if Marty's noticed he's gone yet."

"CC," I said. "Marty might be one of the guys the cops are going to arrest."

"Oh, yeah. Well, he'd still feel better knowing Bob's safe. Maybe he'll let me keep him if they close up the store 'cause he goes to jail."

This was not making me feel better.

I was rescued by Aunt Jenn, calling down from the balcony. "Dunc, I need you. Now."

CHAPTER

Big Time Bounce

Mrs. Ludovic was fretting in the hallway. "Up and dun, up and dun she runnink, Duncan. Iz not good. I am vorried for your auntie."

"I think it's shock," I echoed Wiley Kendall. "Thanks, Mrs. Ludovic."

When I stepped into our apartment the first thing I noticed was cigarette smoke.

"Hey," I said to Aunt Jenn. "Have you been—"

"Never mind that now," said Aunt Jenn. "Just listen."

She was pacing our little living room, still in her workboots. Wiley Kendall stood in the doorway of the kitchenette, peering worriedly at her through his glasses.

"I need you both to do something for me," Aunt Jenn said. "It's important."

"*Ahem*, count on it, Jenn," Wiley Kendall nodded.

She looked at us in turn. "When the police come, I want you to leave Lamar Del Ray out of it."

"Why?" I protested. "He looks like the Borsalino Bandit. He borrowed your car right before that other robbery. And then last week he disappears with Marty Raymond and they get back and—"

"*Disappeared with Marty Raymond?* Skeets, what are you talking about? Never mind, tell me later. There's no time right now. Listen to me: Did you see Lamar Del Ray yesterday?"

"Well, no," I said. "But CC saw the guy, and the description fits. It has to be him."

"*Ahem*, don't think you have to protect that fella, Jenn. Saw him the once and I knew he's no good."

Aunt Jenn ignored Wiley Kendall. "But you didn't actually see him, Dunc? Did you?" I shook my head no. "So you don't really know, do you? So leave him out, don't accuse people you don't know about. Like Wiley said, anybody could have stolen my car, while I was shopping maybe, and then brought it back — if that happened at all."

"Well, *ahem*, if we had a picture of this Lamar to show to CC . . ." Wiley Kendall began.

"There are no pictures," Aunt Jenn snapped.

"Aunt Jenn," I pleaded, "we have to tell them we at least suspect him. And he *is* suspicious. Marty Raymond knows him, and you said Marty Raymond is big trouble. And when I called Aurora B, they said they've never even heard of him, so what's that about? It's suspicious."

"You called Aurora B about him? *You called Aurora B?*" Aunt Jenn pulled off her Sox cap and slammed it to the floor. "Listen, you two, I asked for help: no Lamar Del Ray. That means no questions, no arguments. Will you do that or not?"

"Well, *ahem*, can't say I'm happy about it . . ." Wiley murmured. Aunt Jenn looked fiercely at me.

I said, "I think it's too late."

"What do you mean?"

"I already told his name on the hotline. I thought the police might come faster if I did, seeing as how he has a record, and well, I thought it might help get the reward . . ."

Aunt Jenn covered her face with her hands. "The reward," she said into them.

"To help us," I fumbled, "for school, so you wouldn't have to work so hard."

Aunt Jenn's hands slid down from her eyes till just her mouth was covered. Her eyes were wet. She gusted a huge sigh into her hands, then took them from her face. "How long do we have?"

"Till the police?" Wiley Kendall checked his watch. "A good while yet. Duncan said they were busy."

"Get Marty Raymond," Aunt Jenn said to me. "Get him here now."

I ran to the balcony and yelled to CC. She used her phone, then took off toward the plaza on her bike. Zal stayed with the car. Aunt Jenn lit another cigarette and paced. Wiley Kendall went with Mrs. Ludovic to make coffee.

I stood in the kitchen doorway, filled with a dread that *World's Best* detectives never seemed to get. It looked as if I'd been right all along about Aunt Jenn and Lamar Del Ray. Why else would she want to protect him? And something else had gone wrong, but I didn't know what. All my brain would let me do was notice that Wiley Kendall's broom was leaning beside me. I watched it do nothing for what seemed like a long time but probably wasn't, longing for my Nick Storm mystery instead of this one. Why hadn't I just stuck with it?

Aunt Jenn abruptly came in off the balcony. "They're coming up," she said. She walked over to me. "Skeeter," she said, "give me a hug," and folded me into her arms.

I hugged back and for a second the dread was gone and it was just me and Aunt Jenn like it had been since before I could remember. Then there was a knock at the door and she let me go.

"It's open," she called.

Marty Raymond came into the apartment. CC, Zal, Wiley Kendall and Mrs. Ludovic crowded in behind. Mrs. Ludovic had a tray with coffee things on it.

"You all better be in on this," Aunt Jenn said. "I never wanted it this way; hell, I never wanted it at all, but now there's no time for anything else."

She nodded at Marty Raymond. "Duncan," Aunt Jenn said, "meet Lamar Del Ray. He's also your father."

Believe-It-or-Not Bounce

think Mrs. Ludovic dropped the tray but I'm not sure.
Nobody else moved. I thought I was still breathing.

Marty Raymond said, "You changed your mind. I'm
grateful."

"I didn't change my mind. Things have changed,"
Aunt Jenn snapped.

The words were like another language. I tried to find
my own. All I got was, "Who . . . My dad is Bill . . . his
fishparents drowned."

"That was a story they made up for you," Marty Raymond said. "Truth is, I'm your dad. Lamar Del Ray is my
real name. I was young and stupid when your mom told
me she was expecting. I panicked and run off. It was a
sorry thing to do. And later, after I learned she'd died, I

tried to get in touch with your folks, but no one would tell me anything 'cept you'd been told I was dead too and to stay away. But after I did my time, I came looking. I found your Aunt Jenn here and the store for rent in the plaza and I knew it had to be. Those were my two dreams, see: finding you and starting Gator Aid."

Zal interrupted, "So you went to jail for smuggling baby turtles in your sweatpants, not for a Madagascar plowshare tortoise."

"'Fraid so, pardner." Marty sighed. "I started calling myself Marty Raymond so people in the business wouldn't connect me with the smuggling. I was kind of on the dark side then. I know this is all hard to take in. I'll show you my passport if you want."

"Already saw it," said CC. Marty Raymond's brow wrinkled.

I cut in, "But Lamar Del— He was here. I *met* him. I saw—"

"That wasn't Lamar Del Ray," Aunt Jenn cut in. She looked at all of us. Her chin tilted up and you could see the tornado starting in her eyes. "That was me."

Maybe that was when Mrs. Ludovic dropped the tray. Either way, coffee was pooling around our feet on the parquet floor. No one cared.

"That man you saw," Aunt Jenn went on, "he doesn't exist. It was me in disguise: a wig and a beard and a pillow on my middle. That's why Aurora B never heard of him. I dressed up and brought Wiley's delivery here to test it out. If you'd recognized me, I'd never have gone through with it. I'd have said I was just fooling around for a costume party at work. I didn't expect you to ask my name, but when you did, I blurted one that went with trouble. It was just coincidence that the real Lamar showed up. I didn't even recognize him then, not until I saw his close-up on TV when you caught the alligator. I'd thought we'd never see him again." She turned to Marty/ Lamar. "I didn't intend for you to get dragged in."

Her chin came down and the storm blew out in her eyes. Then she said, "Sorry."

"Trouble?" said Marty/Lamar.

"Gone through with what?" That was Wiley Kendall.

"Robbing banks," said Aunt Jenn. "It was the only way to pay Dunc's school fees. I'm the Borsalino Bandit."

That was definitely when Mrs. Ludovic fainted. Marty/ Lamar and Wiley Kendall helped her onto the couch.

"So, here's the thing," Aunt Jenn said. "I've just confessed. The police are coming. You can turn me in, get the reward; one of you, all of you. Or you can break the law and help send Duncan to school."

CHAPTER

Baby Bounce

I'm not saying what we did next was right. I'm just saying we did it. I think CC and Zal thought it was more
exciting than getting the reward.

Anyway, everybody pitched in. Mrs. Ludovic cleaned
up the coffee spill. Aunt Jenn gathered up some things.
CC, Zal, Wiley Kendall and I agreed on what we'd say,
which was mostly what happened with no Lamar Del
Ray. Marty/Lamar listened. Then Wiley Kendall took
a garbage bag with the things Aunt Jenn had gathered,
mostly her disguise gear, down behind the building and
stuffed it deep in the garbage bins out back. It would be
gone with the next day's pickup.

CC and Zal went out to the car to check on Bob and
let us know when the cops arrived. That left Marty/

Lamar, Aunt Jenn and me. My family, strange to think. We looked at each other.

"Listen, Jenn, Duncan," Marty/Lamar said. "About the money, I have to tell you—"

"The money stays where it is," said Aunt Jenn. Her chin came up again. "And never mind where that is. Duncan goes to school no matter what." She resisted lighting another cigarette.

"That's not what I meant," Marty/Lamar said. "I meant, I know I have a lot to make up for." Aunt Jenn snorted and lit her cigarette after all. I waved smoke away. Marty/Lamar kept right on. "So, when you told me — yelled at me — about Duncan and school a few weeks back, I did something about it."

I braced myself to hear that he'd been robbing banks too, but Marty/Lamar said, "I just got back a couple days ago. Brokered a deal on a sunglow ball python that I got a line on; a colour morph."

"Were you smuggling again?" I asked.

"No way, straight commission deal for a client, strictly legit." He shrugged, "'Cept I might not've said it was a colour morph on the customs form. Knew the guy on duty didn't care for snakes."

"I heard you say on the phone that ball pythons are cheap."

"Not colour morphs, pardner. They're specially bred, rarest of the rare. This baby went for thirty-eight thousand dollars. My share was five grand, plus what I saved on customs. That's why I was so happy Thursday. I'm giving it to you two for Duncan's school. It's a start, anyway."

My family. My crime family.

"We don't need your money." Aunt Jenn blew more smoke.

"Yes we do," I said. "You can't keep on . . ." I waved my hand, partly to finish what I was saying without saying it, and partly to keep the smoke away.

Aunt Jenn shot me a laser-beam look. "I'll do whatever it takes."

"Then I'll just give it to Duncan," Marty/Lamar said. "You can't shut me out forever."

Aunt Jenn's shoulders slumped. "Okay, you're both right." She looked at Marty/Lamar. "Thank you. It is a start. Let's just deal with this first."

Her cellphone buzzed. It was Zal.

"They're coming up."

CHAPTER

Back Pocket Bounce

"They" were Zal, CC, Wiley Kendall and Sergeant Castro. He didn't look happy to see me. "Duncan Fortune," he said, around his gum. "We meet again. You're a persistent young man, Duncan. I hope it pays off, for all of us."

"Hi, Sergeant. How's Detective Yee?" Suddenly I was so nervous that polite was all that came out. I guess Aunt Jenn had trained me well.

"She's fine. She's downstairs with the car." His glance flicked over all of us and came to rest on the big broom.

"Oh. That's, uh, mine," Wiley Kendall said. "Wondered where I left it."

"Uh-huh," said Sergeant Castro. He looked at us again. Everyone shifted uneasily. "Does this involve all of you?"

143

"Well, I guess it does, one way or another," said Aunt Jenn. "We surely hope you can help us, Sergeant. This morning I found a snake in my car, frightened the life out of me, and now my nephew Duncan and his friends think it means my car was used in a bank robbery. I just don't know what's going on."

"I know the feeling," Sergeant Castro said, chewing. It didn't look as if Aunt Jenn was going to get him shuffling and *ahem*ing. "But I'm hoping this may save me interviewing the clairvoyant who claims to have visions of where the loot is." He looked at me. "I'm not holding my breath. All right, Duncan, let's start with you. Take your time."

I went through it the way we'd planned: how Zal, CC and I were trying to catch the Borsalino Bandit to get the reward and help our families with school fees, how we'd figured out a pattern to the robberies (I let Zal explain that part; the sergeant was impressed), how we'd staked out the plaza but only CC had seen what happened.

Then CC described the man she saw walk into the bank, and how she'd run out from Gator Aid and dumped Bob into the robber's car. She said she didn't know the kind of car, but the licence had been something like AW5. Marty/Lamar said he ran the business but had been out at the time and got back just after and that Bob was indeed gone. "Lamar Del Ray," he introduced himself. "But I run the store as Marty Raymond."

"Duncan named a Lamar Del Ray in his message," said Sergeant Castro. "That you? He seems to think you did it."

"I got confused because I was excited," I said quickly. "I was trying to say CC thought the robber looked like him."

"Okay," Sergeant Castro said. "So, CC here put a snake in the robber's car, whatever it was. How come the robber didn't flip out? I, personally, would go through the roof."

"Either the dude didn't mind snakes," said Marty/ Lamar, "or, more likely, 'ol Bob headed right under the nearest seat. Milk snakes are hiders."

"And now there's a snake in Ms. Fortune's car." Sergeant Castro turned to Aunt Jenn. "Where was your car yesterday, Ms. Fortune, and where were you?"

"I took it to work at Aurora B Nurseries," said Aunt Jenn. "I was there all day, except when I took a late lunch and drove over to Woodside Market to do our shopping. I was working overtime — it's that time of year — and I knew I'd be too tired after."

"What time did you shop?"

"Around two, I think. It took a while. It was a big shop."

"It was," Wiley Kendall agreed. "I helped her bring it in."

"You went straight to the grocery from work?"

Aunt Jenn nodded. "It's not far."

"And your car was unattended in the lot while you shopped. How long?"

Aunt Jenn shrugged. "Forty minutes? Like I said, it was a load."

"Was it locked?"

"Probably not. I know I should. Still have some small town in me, I guess."

Sergeant Castro folded his arms across his chest, considering. "The robbery was around two-twenty. Woodside's six or seven minutes away, tops. Someone could steal your car, use it for the robbery and return it before you even knew it was gone. Stranger things have happened. Let's have a look at the car."

Outside, it was already almost as hot as the day before had been. Detective Yee was in the unmarked cruiser, parked behind Aunt Jenn's twined-off Toyota. She got out and nodded to us.

Sergeant Castro said, "We have a partial plate number, AW5." Detective Yee jotted it down. We all looked at Aunt Jenn's licence: *OKG 853*.

"This one is registered to a Jennifer Anne Fortune, of this address," said Detective Yee, nodding at the plate.

"Well, yes, that would be me," said Aunt Jenn.

"This the car?" Sergeant Castro asked CC.

She shrugged. "It was *like* this. I only know trucks. These all look the same."

"You're not alone. We had witnesses say Toyota, Honda, Nissan and, believe it or not, a Hummer." Sergeant Castro stepped over the twine and peered in the car. He drew back quickly and turned to CC and Marty/Lamar. "How about the snake? Geez, it looks like a rattler."

"*Milk* snake," CC snorted. "They're harmless."

Marty/Lamar said, "Can I?" and pointed at the twine.

"*May* I," CC corrected.

Zal and I glared at her.

"Go ahead," said Sergeant Castro. They both stepped over the twine and looked in, CC right behind.

"Hey, Bob," said CC. "Snakes I know."

Shut up, I thought.

"Well, it is a milk snake," said Marty/Lamar. "Can't say if it's Bob. The markings don't differentiate enough, you know? And snakes often get into strange places on their own. I took one of these out of a house near here a while back. In the dryer, came in through the vent."

"Geez," Sergeant Castro grimaced. "They common around here?"

"There'll be a few. Not much habitat in the city. They eat rodents, mostly, so definitely some in Oakwood Park."

"Been there lately, Ms. Fortune?"

"A few days ago," Aunt Jenn picked up on Marty/Lamar's lead. "I take my lunch there if I have the time."

"They can go a spell without eating," Marty/Lamar followed up. "Like I said, be happy as a clam under your seats."

Aunt Jenn shuddered. "That thing could have been in there all this time?"

Sergeant Castro chewed harder, maybe thinking about his own car. Then he got back to business. "So, Ms. Fortune's car is probable, right size and colour and could have been stolen at the right time to be the robbery vehicle, but we can't confirm make or model and the plates are different. There *is* a snake inside, but we can't positively ID it either and it could have been there a while, so the whole thing could be a coincidence. A strange one, but they happen."

He looked at Detective Yee. She shrugged. He looked at his watch. For the first time, I had the feeling we were going to get away with it.

"Well," Sergeant Castro said, "I think we're about done for now. You've all been helpful. Ms. Fortune, could we just wrap this up with a look in the back of the car?"

Aunt Jenn blinked. "Go right on, it's not locked. I haven't had it open. I put the groceries in the back seat to take into Aurora B. It is a mess, though."

We huddled at the back of the car as Sergeant Castro took a packet of latex gloves from his jacket pocket. He snapped them on and raised the hatchback. Inside was our usual jumble of junk: jumper cables, motor oil and washer fluid, an old blanket, a milk crate stuffed with plastic bags, some planter flats from Aurora B, a sweatshirt I'd been looking for. Sergeant Castro poked around, then lifted a corner of the blanket. Something was underneath.

He shifted things gently and lifted the blanket higher.

There was a licence plate: AHW 055.

We all gasped.

"I'll run it, contact the owner," said Detective Yee. She shook her head as she turned to the cruiser. "Sometimes people don't notice. We all take them for granted."

"Find out if they were at or near Woodside Market yesterday," called Sergeant Castro. To us, he said, "Looks as if he switched your plate with one he stole, from the same parking lot, I'll bet. A double blind. Didn't have time to ditch it, or he didn't care. Look here, here, here." Sergeant Castro pointed at the bottom of the trunk, the stolen plate and the blanket. There were flecks of bright red-orange paint, almost the colour of Zal's bouncy ball. He lifted my sweatshirt. It was smeared with the stuff. He knelt and peered at Aunt Jenn's licence plate. "And here too, little specks. The teller slipped a dye pack in with the stolen money. The robber must have got it on himself too."

"So somebody stole my car," Aunt Jenn whispered.

Sergeant Castro nodded, stood up and swiped at his knee. "Looks like this is the vehicle. Ms. Fortune, we'll have to leave this car as is for the tech folks to sweep. I wonder if we could just go back upstairs so I can organize my notes and ask you a last couple of questions?"

I went back up with Sergeant Castro and Aunt Jenn. The others stayed in the parking lot. Sergeant Castro asked Aunt Jenn to go over the times she left work and went shopping. He made more notes.

"This is one thorough crook," he said, flipping his notebook shut. "Changing plates on a stolen car."

"If Aunt Jenn came back early and her car was gone," I pointed out, "she'd report it. He wouldn't want you guys watching for it if he was going to rob a bank." It was the kind of extra-sneaky thing criminals would do in *World's Best*.

Sergeant Castro nodded slowly. "Good point. Keep your career choices open, Duncan. You might make detective. In the meantime, I'd better get on this. Thank you for your help. This is our first break in the case. The tech team will be over later and I'll be in touch. Sorry for the inconvenience." He handed Aunt Jenn his card. "If you think of anything else, let me know right away."

We'd done it. Aunt Jenn led us to the door. "I don't know which gives me the willies more," she said, over her shoulder, "having my car stolen by a bank robber, or driving around with a snake in it."

Sergeant Castro didn't answer. He was looking at Aunt Jenn's rear end. Her leather work gloves were crammed into her back pocket. One was streaked with glowing red-orange paint.

As she turned to face us, he said, "Some crooks switch plates on a stolen car. Not many switch them back again. Ms. Fortune, I'm going to ask you to come down to the station."

Biggest Bounce

Aunt Jenn confessed. She didn't rat us out for helping; a Fortune always takes one for the team. The prosecutor asked for ten years and said Aunt Jenn was robbing banks in revenge for B&G Trust firing her. But when Aunt Jenn's lawyer got the story out that she was really doing it to afford to send me to Studies Institute, the tables turned. Some of Aunt Jenn's old bank customers even gave interviews about how great she was. The folks at Aurora B said they'd hold her job for her. *What Mother Wouldn't?* read one headline.

Suddenly Aunt Jenn was some kind of hero. In the end, the judge said the whole thing was obviously out of character and stress-related, and she'd never had a weapon or threatened anyone and he believed she'd make up for her mistakes. He gave her five years, eligible for parole in three, less time already served. *What Mother Wouldn't* indeed?

The police found most of the stolen money in shoeboxes in our basement storage locker. It wasn't hard to find. The money had to be given back, of course, including what Aunt Jenn had paid the school, so I lost my tuition. The money Marty made on the python sale went to pay Aunt Jenn's lawyer, and it turned out the bursary was really money she stole too. But the publicity made other things happen. People started a trust fund for my education. We donated the money to a charity for underprivileged kids.

That's because I decided not to go to Studies Institute after all. I'm back at Park Lawn. Miss Linton changed grades with me, so I have her for this year too. That's fine with me. I like Miss Linton, and besides, I'd had just about all the change I could handle then. That was one reason Lamar Del Ray and I agreed that I'd call him Marty, the way I'd thought of him before. *Dad* was too weird and Marty says he likes it better than Lamar anyway.

Marty and I stayed in the apartment too. It's convenient to Gator Aid. Marty and Wiley Kendall get on pretty well, now that Wiley Kendall knows Marty isn't chasing after Aunt Jenn. Every so often, Mrs. Ludovic has us both over for dinner. Marty gave her an iguana, the brother of Betty, the one he'd sold in the shop. Mrs.

Ludovic loves it. It turns out she was a wildlife biologist in her own country before she came here. She named the iguana Boris.

In fact, of the three of us, only Zal ended up going to SI. CC's dad got a new job up north where they went to camp and fish, and the whole family moved at the end of summer. We keep in touch online. Next summer, she wants to be a counsellor at a big camp up there. She's also stuffing a raccoon. You don't want to see the in-progress pictures. I still hang with Zal. He got his batting average up to .200. He has a big talent show audition coming up.

Me, I'm busy, helping out at the store. I never did write *Bad Bounce*. I wrote this instead. It seemed even stranger than anything I could make up. It was also a deal of work and I'm glad it's done. Miss Linton is looking for an idea for our class play, though, so *Bad Bounce* might get written yet. I have another idea too.

For the first few months I didn't see Aunt Jenn. Marty, Wiley Kendall and Mrs. Ludovic did, and a bunch of other people. I didn't want to go see her in jail. I didn't want to see her anywhere else either, truth to tell. I knew she'd robbed the banks for me, but that just made it feel as if the whole thing was my fault. I didn't want to feel that. Like I said, enough had already changed.

Finally, Marty took me out there. He said it wasn't a high-security jail, but it looked secure enough to me. Marty waited for me outside the visiting area. Aunt Jenn and I sat in a room where a bunch of other families were visiting too. The tables and swivel chairs were bolted to the floor and walls, like in a fast food restaurant. We sat side by side. I didn't want to look her in the eye.

"How are you, Skeets?" she said. Her red hair was cut short. She had on an orange jumpsuit. It was too big.

I looked at the table.

"Fine. Good. Okay. Marty sent you cigarettes."

"Thank him for me, but I've quit again. School's good?"

"Okay. Miss Linton says hi." I didn't want to talk about school. School had gotten us here in the first place. I said, "How's jail?"

I could feel her winding up for some kind of cheery comment, but finally she just said, "Okay. Fine. Good." She sighed. "It sucks, Duncan. I hate it here."

"What did you do it for?" There, it was out.

"I had a dream for you."

"Don't say it was for me! It wasn't my dream." I clung tight to the seat of my plastic chair. The tabletop had little gold flecks in it.

"You don't know yet how much there is to dream about, hon."

"But you wrecked *everything*." The gold flecks got blurry. I fought to keep my voice from wobbling.

"I changed everything. Maybe it was time." She jogged me with her elbow, our first touch. "*You* wrecked everything."

"Me?"

"You caught me."

I turned to Aunt Jenn. Her lips twitched the faintest almost-smile. "There's not many can say that. And I'll tell you something else, a secret. Just you and me. I've been thinking a lot since I got here. There's another reason I did it. It was plain wrong and it was stupid, but truth to tell, there was a little thrill. It was fun. Maybe I needed a change too."

I kind of glugged, giggled and hiccupped all at the same time. Aunt Jenn smiled sadly.

"Just sayin', Skeets. I did a bad thing and I hate that; I can't help it if I liked it too. Just a smidge. If I'd really been doing it just for you, I wouldn't have done it. It wasn't your fault. I think I did it for me too. Maybe you can't understand."

I sniffed. "I think I do. What will we do when you get out?"

She gave me a hug then. I hugged her back.

"You know Aurora B says I can have my job back when I get out. Those folks are good to me."

"If you want it," I said. "Maybe it will be time for something different."

Aunt Jenn hugged me tighter. "Maybe it will. I've got a little for a rainy day. We'll see when it's time."

I guessed we would. There'd be a lot to see about, but I figured I'd be ready.

I almost forgot: If you're wondering, we got the reward. Zal was relieved, let me tell you. His share helped with his school fees, even though it was nowhere near enough. CC bought some stuff and gave some to the kids charity. I didn't feel right, collecting a reward for catching my own aunt, so I gave my share to the charity too.

Besides, Aunt Jenn had said she had a little for a rainy day. At first I didn't understand exactly what she meant. Then one Saturday, doing my eight-plex chores, I bumped Wiley Kendall's broom as I was putting the mop back in the caretaker closet. The broom handle gave a dull clunk as it hit the floor. I stared at it. I slipped into the closet, turned on the light and pulled the door shut. It was a job of work to get that handle off, but I did it. One end of a piece of string was taped inside.

I pulled. Out came rolls of hundred-dollar bills, paper-clipped to the string. I counted twice: there were thirty bills — three thousand dollars. Wiley Kendall always said he was wily by name not by nature, so I knew they weren't his. I put everything back the way I'd found it and got out of there.

Marty took me to see Aunt Jenn again a week later. By then I'd thought it all out. We talked about this and that.

"Zal says hi," I told her.

"How is Zal?" Aunt Jenn looked tired. Her freckles stood out.

"He's okay. He asked me if Wiley Kendall needs any

more helpers. I think his family is worried about keeping on paying for Studies Institute."

"Don't we know about that. It's a darn shame. Did you ask Wiley?"

"I'm going to. I need the help. I was so tired, I dropped his big broom the other day." I looked out the barred window. "Made a big clunk. Like in my mystery."

I kept on watching clouds.

Aunt Jenn didn't say anything. I watched more clouds. She still didn't say anything. I risked a look. She was staring at me. Her face was dead pale except for the freckles. Was a tornado brewing? She turned to the window. I wondered if she was looking at the bars or the sky.

When Aunt Jenn turned back, her eyes were clear.

"I remember that, Skeeter. I'll leave it with you. You'll know what to do." Then she smiled, one of her big ones. It was the first wrap-around, catch the wrong train, sinka-phone on a psychedelic truck, haunted house Aunt Jenn smile I'd seen in ages.

"You know," she said, "I had a headache when I came in here and now it's gone." She looked out the window again. "I do believe it's not going to rain."

It wasn't very hard to do. After all, I'd picked up a few tricks from *World's Best*. I addressed a bunch of envelopes to Zal's house, using different pens and printing, and different computer fonts. Then I split the money into unequal amounts and put some in each envelope, wrapped in a note with matching printing that said, "For your school," or "A donation for your education," but with no name. I sealed the envelopes, and every time Marty took a road trip for Gator Aid I'd get him to mail one from a different place. They never found out where the money came from, and don't you tell.

It was an easy job but I got a little thrill out of doing it in secret. I know it made Zal's family happy. For me and Aunt Jenn, I think that was the biggest thrill of all.

Appendix One
Surviving the Zombie Apocalypse

The English section of the SI exam had two parts. One was paragraphs of a story, with blanks where you were supposed to guess and fill in the missing words. That was pretty easy. The other was an essay question, with three topics to choose from. Like I said, I picked *Describe and explain the best way to survive the zombie apocalypse.* This was something CC, Zal and I had talked over a lot.

I said you'd do best taking off for the woods in a team of three. You'd have one person who knew about wilderness survival, one fighter and one tech person for when you returned later to what remained of civilization. You'd need camp stuff, a gun and ammo, batteries, an axe, a shovel (both also good for chopping zombie heads off), a first-aid kit and lots of books to read while you waited.

And waiting is the key part. See, if you hid in the woods a few years, sooner or later there wouldn't be any people left to either be zombie food or to make new zombies. This is important, because most people don't realize it, but zombies don't last forever. Since they're already dead, they keep on rotting and bits fall off. Sooner or later, when enough bits have fallen off, they won't be able to do anything. When there are no new ones and the old ones aren't dangerous anymore, you just come out of the woods and sweep up. I got right into all that and had to hurry to finish at the end. Afterwards, we all got burgers for lunch.

I'm not saying it is super-genius stuff, but if you write the SI exam and that question turns up, feel free to use this. I'm pretty sure it helped me, and I hope it helps you too. And if you do get into SI, watch out for the tuna noodle hot lunch. Zal says Sergeant Castro was right.

Appendix Two
Bad Bounce

Now that I have written something all the way to the end, I can tell you as an author that, for my money, the toughest part is figuring out where to start. Here are four different ways I tried to start *Bad Bounce*. I was also trying to sound like the writing in *World's Best*, if it sounds different than my usual.

~~It wasn't often that Inspector Chase of the Yard called on Nick Storm, so when~~ **When** Carruthers the butler ushered ~~him~~ **Inspector Chase** into Nick's ~~sweet~~ **suite** at Claridge's, the great detective instantly knew *at once that* adventure was afoot.

Over the years, ~~the master criminal~~ Kendali, **the king of crime,** had stolen a king's ransom in jewels, but no one had ever seen his face, only the mocking notes he left at the scenes of his astonishing crimes. Inspector Chase passed the newest one to Nick Storm. The keen-eyed detective read it and handed it to me. "What do you make of it, Fortune?"

At first glance it seemed all too oblivious: the alarm off, the broken glass of the museum display case strewed throughout the floor, with the broom of the caretaker who had been knocked cold during the robbery. The caretaker himself was nursing his battered brow and the priceless Lamar diamonds were gone. But Nick Storm's ~~sensitive~~ detecting sense told him something ~~was amiss. was wrong.~~ **_wasn't right._**

Afterwards, when pressed to tell his tale at the Sleuth Club, Nick Storm would always say the whole case came down to knowing ~~one word~~ _two things_: Zectron. ~~That and not being so good at a school game called~~ _and a game called_ wall ball.

If you can finish any of these, go for it. Like I said, Miss Linton is looking for a story for our class play, but I have a new idea I like better, with more action. I'm calling it _The Green Pond Gator Mystery_. It's about three friends who rescue animals, only one is scared of dogs and one carries turtles in her pockets everywhere. First they get a giant anaconda out of a clothes dryer and then they wrangle a giant alligator in a city pond and try to figure out how it got there. The special effects could be spectacular. Good luck. See you at the beach.

Acknowledgements

For me, acknowledgements are always fun and frightening. It's great to give a shout-out to everyone who helped, but I'm always scared I'm going to accidentally leave someone out. I'll do my best not to mess up.

First off, I'd like to thank herpetologist extraordinaire Lee Parker, of Reptilia, in Vaughan, Ontario, who really did wrangle a caiman out of a pond in Toronto's High Park, barehanded. Lee generously shared his knowledge and experiences, and parts of my story owe a lot to him. You can see Lee in action if you do a web search for "High Park Alligator." Thanks also to his colleagues at Reptilia, who patiently answered many silly questions, including "what would happen if an anaconda swallowed a wad of twenty-dollar bills?" And still on this topic, I'd be more than remiss if I didn't thank Michele McKenzie of Sutton District Library for her energy and enthusiasm in connecting me with everyone at Reptilia. Her help really got things happening with this book.

Lee and company are the good guys in the reptile side of the story. The bad guy bits were inspired by news reports and a funny, fascinating book, *Stolen Worlds*, by Jennie

Erin Smith, about the bizarre world of reptile smugglers and smuggling. It's a fun read.

As for the bank robbery side, thanks to Kim Armstrong at my local bank branch for insight into what tellers are trained to do in a robbery, as well as numerous news stories, especially "The Last Ride of Cowboy Bob," a moving piece of reporting by Skip Hollandsworth in *The Best American Crime Writing 2006*.

Over in the imagining corner, I have to mention Miss Linton, Miss Hart, Mr. Lowe, Mrs. Ross and all the other teachers at the real Park Lawn School, who did such cool, arts-based stuff with me and all their other students way back when, not to mention Mom and Dad for countless trips to the library, family stories (mostly true), and for visits to the long-vanished book and antique shop near Rice Lake — where I bought my four precious (and incredibly cheesy) time-capsule volumes of the ten-volume *The World's Best 100 Detective Stories* with painstakingly saved paper-route money. Fifty cents a book. It seemed like a fortune, but it was a great investment.

Thanks also to Jeremy, Liz and Karla of Mabel's Fables, in Toronto, who led me on an illuminating web search and discussion about bouncy balls, their history and related games one spring afternoon.

As for the nuts and bolts of writing and business, I'm again indebted to David Bennett for guiding this project safely into port at Scholastic. His story sense was a big help too.

Next, a huge thanks to my editor, Anne Shone, for her faith in this story, her insights and (not least) her humour. Anne has a way of making you write precisely what you thought you already had, but were really only gesturing at vaguely. If she'd edited that last sentence, for example, it would be a lot clearer. Thanks also to Aldo Fierro for a great cover, Erin Haggett for fastidious fact checking and attention to detail, and everyone on the Scholastic team for their energy, enthusiasm and talents in getting this book to you.

Last, but never least, thanks to Margaret and Will, who keep the bounce in my step and my heart.

ABOUT THE AUTHOR

Patricia McCaw

Ted **Staunton** is the prize-winning author of many
books for young people, from long-time picture book
favourite *Puddleman*, to young adult and middle-grade
novels, including *Who I'm Not* and titles in the bestselling
Seven series. He's also a popular speaker who has performed
and led workshops everywhere from Inuvik to Addis Ababa.
When not writing stories, Ted writes music and plays in the
Maple Leaf Champions Jug Band. Ted lives with his family
in Port Hope, Ontario.